I0634438

Amanda H. Ferry Hall

Within, Without and Over

Or Memorials of the Earnest Life of Henry Clay Hal...

Amanda H. Ferry Hall

Within, Without and Over
Or Memorials of the Earnest Life of Henry Clay Hal...

ISBN/EAN: 9783337267438

Printed in Europe, USA, Canada, Australia, Japan

Cover: Foto ©Raphael Reischuk / pixelio.de

More available books at **www.hansebooks.com**

WITHIN, WITHOUT, AND OVER,

OR

MEMORIALS OF THE EARNEST LIFE

OF

HENRY CLAY HALL,

LAYMAN,

WHO ENTERED INTO REST FROM HIS RESIDENCE IN
NEW YORK CITY, APRIL 12, 1873,
AGED FORTY-FIVE YEARS.

"For so He giveth His beloved sleep."

NORTHAMPTON, MASS. :
BRIDGMAN & CHILDS.
1878.

Knowing his deeds of love, men questioned not
The faith of one whose walk and word were right,—
Who tranquilly in life's great task-field wrought.
And, side by side with evil, scarcely caught
A stain upon his pilgrim-garb of white.

—Whittier.

Fame is the perfume of noble deeds.—*Socrates.*

Great peace have they which love thy Law ; and nothing
shall offend them.—*Psalm of David.*

For nearly five years the compiler of these pages has hesitated to make this public record. But a request urged when death arrested such valued and untiring activities, has been often repeated by men of experience and influence, who knew how to prize christian integrity in the life so fairly tested,—and their importunity must be the shield under which the " work " is offered.

" It will not be long—be brave and bear it ; do my work with yours, while you stay,—*and I will do all a spirit can to help you.*"

Though spoken as a sacred private benediction, may these parting words of him whose sun went down at meridian, but whose life was long as we measure results, linger like an inspiration throughout these pages, that *young men*, who were the peculiar interest of the departed, may learn what a single-hearted, unassuming layman, through a pure and consecrated life, may do—for the Master and for the world.

BITTER-SWEET LODGE,
    May, 1878.

CONTENTS.

WITHIN, WITHOUT, AND OVER.

I.

Boyhood.

The fair face of a musing boy,
   * * * * with graceful flow
Of boyhood's soft and waving hair
   And fresh young lip, and cheek, and brow,
Unmarked and clear, were there ;
   Yet through its sweet and calm repose
I saw the inward spirit shine ;
   It was as if before me rose
The white veil of a shrine.—*Whittier*.

Remembrance is the only paradise out of which we cannot be driven away.—*Richter*.

TWELVE miles westward from the station at South Deerfield of the Connecticut River Railway, or nine miles northwesterly from the terminus of the New Haven and Northampton road at Williamsburg, or eight miles southerly from Shelburne Falls on the Hoosac Valley line, the tourist may reach, through ever changing, often picturesque, and sometimes grand mountain scenery, the quiet village of Ashfield.

Here, in later years, remote from the active centers of progress, literary and scientific men find a charming summer retreat. Here, in the pure dry air of an elevation two hundred feet above the crest of Mt. Holyoke, and twelve hundred feet above the level of the sea, invalids find an unfailing tonic ; and in the walks and drives stretching every whither over this watershed of a southern spur of the Green Mountain chain, and which a visitor, long resident in Palestine, recently pronounced the nearest resemblance he had found on this continent to the scenery around Galilee, they may find a perpetual recreation and joy.

To others, this retired neighborhood with its peaceful lake nestled among the sheltering hills like a jewel in setting of emerald, has become by long years of residence or ownership, *a saint's rest.* Some such sit now beside the ancestral firesides, where generations have been welcomed to the ample warmth and cheer. Each passing year " brings them nearer to the Master's glorious face," but while they hasten to wear the shining garments,—and the light of the celestial city even now encircles with radiance their placid brows — they linger tenderly over the sacred memories of the past; and among these, over the times when Sanderson Academy — the leading school of the region, the consecrated gift of its founder and name-sake, and the just pride of its supporters — trained and developed as teachers or pupils such minds as Edwards the theologian, Loomis the mathematician, Burritt and Clark the astronomers, Gillette the philanthropist, Fowler the phrenologist, Aldrich the jurist, Mary Lyon the teacher, King the missionary — and Paine, Porter, Brigham, Alden, White, Ferry, Bement, Smith, Sears, Williams, and others of like aim, who went out thence "in the dew of their youth," well furnished for useful service, and are now gathered to their reward.

In the decadence of these brighter days, in one of the pleasant homes of this mountain village, Henry Clay Hall began his earthly life. In the same Academy, Dawes, Mitchell, and Wilder, developed his vigorous mind. In a social atmosphere well charged with healthy qualities, he grew and thrived. Nature, too, invited him to her rarest festivals, and he was her constant, familiar, admiring guest. His fellowship with birds and flowers, with rocks and streams, with the broad basking-grounds of the sweet meadows,

and with the mysterious shades and symphonies
of the mossy woods, was an unfailing source of
delight and strength.   At the age of fourteen,
shouldering his surveying instruments, he began
a series of land and road surveys through the
unexplored marshes and heavy timber-growths of
his own and adjoining towns.   This pastime he
keenly relished, and in later years these were his
favorite resorts and drives.

His home was his choicest training school.
His mother — one of "the lovely Miss Good-
wins"— traced her maternal lineage to the martyr at Smithfield.   His father, descended through
a line of sterling qualities for five generations,
as the records at Yarmouth testify, claimed also
on the maternal side, kinship to the hero of
Bunker-Hill.   Through this double infusion of
patriot and puritan stock, their first child doubtless received the granite foundations of his character.

His patriotism exceeded by far the average
standard for boys.   From his tenth to his four-
teenth years, no fiction fascinated him like the
speeches of Webster and Clay.   These, with the
political columns of the New York and Boston
journals, were a portion of his daily food; and

he not only read them with his father at home,
who was a strong and active whig, but with his
venerable friend, Esquire W., to whom he hastened
evening after evening during exciting political
contests, with all that was eloquent or that fired
his enthusiasm.

He was not a "goody" boy, but he was healthy
in body and in mind, so that, though he was
ready for a large share in neighborhood sports,
the animal exhuberance so common to boy-life
was kept within bounds of decorum by the high
code of honor transmitted from his parents, and
cordially accepted as his own. This was a well
established fact. Some persons yet living in that
village remember that an element of mischief
projected into the leaders of boy-tactics, broke
out one season into nightly pranks of a doubtful
nature. Horses were let loose in their stalls;
window-blinds were removed and hidden from
dwellings; the village flag-staff was laid low;
and, not to enumerate all the list of petty annoy-
ances, each order-loving citizen awoke one morning
to find not only his gates unhinged and missing,
but his gardens nearly demolished by truant cows.
An hour later, while Judge P. and Esquire W.
were looking up the matter in neighborly fashion

with those who chose to join them at the street
corner, a man from an out-lying district stopped
in passing, to say, "Well, whoever did this mischief, we all know of one boy who *did n't* have a
hand in it, and that is Henry Hall.　There's
lots of fun in him, any day, but his fun is all
open and above-board."

Here was the key-note of his life.　Whatever
he undertook was done with his might,— *but it
was "all open and above-board."*

The most remarkable feature of his youth, was
his lover-like devotion, "as a true knight", to
his mother.　No social magnet was strong enough
to lure him long from her side.　Her graceful
and refining ministries illumined his home with
perpetual attractions.　They read and studied and
recreated together as of one mind and soul.
When he was seven years old, his little sister
of rare beauty and precocious mind, whom he
ardently loved, faded as such blossoms often fade,
and in her fifth year "was transplanted to a
more congenial state."　A printed memorial—just
quoted—again says of her: "I have often thought
on seeing her, of those little children whom our
Divine Redeemer took in His arms and blessed,
and I doubt not she resembled them in her

infantile character." This loss was to him an abiding sorrow,—and as one by one, three of the seven children who shared with him the atmosphere of that home were taken to the home enduring, the eldest son charged himself with increased privilege of filial tenderness and care. In after years he looked back upon that home as an earthly paradise.

He delighted to review his mother's tact and wisdom in the training of her family. When he was only ten years old, he surprised her one day with a lighted cigar. Playfully claiming consent to smoke it in her presence, he added : "Other boys smoke, and I think it is quite time for me to begin." "Very well, my son — go on,"— was the calm reply. A few puffs satisfied his curiosity, and not meeting the opposition he had expected, the charm was gone, and he laid the cigar aside. She at once returned it to him, saying firmly, but with a roguish twinkle in her eye "Finish it, Henry." First his pride and then his loyalty was challenged, and he smoked on, till, pale and helpless, she supported him to his room, *entirely cured* as she expected. That was his last cigar.

From fifteen to seventeen, he went through the

course of study at Williston Seminary, leaving a record of marked ability in mathematics. During his sixteenth year he was called home to receive the weight of the heaviest shadow that ever rested on his heart. From that date onward, he was never known to mention the name of his mother without emotion. That anniversary was always sacredly kept. In September, 1853, he wrote from his home in New York:

"A mother nine years in Heaven! I go back to the place, the time. In that upper room, my dearest earthly friend, my idolized mother, is calmly waiting death. I am folded for the last time to the breast that had so often pillowed my aching head. Words burning with life's deepest affection come in whispers across her lips, as she tells me of her intercessions for her darling boy,—that I might be kept from sin, going forth from the parental roof. Even now, her voice swells along the chambers of my soul like the voice of an angel, as with her last breath she directed me to her Saviour, and urged me to seek Him as my best friend for this life, and for the life to come. *I thank my God for such a mother!*"

IN SEPTEMBER, 1856.—"Twelve years to-day, since the first great sorrow of my life. A mother's prayers have pillowed me till now. 'Even to the third and fourth generation of them that love me and keep my commandments' still stand sure. May our lives be such that those who come after us, may inherit that promise."

IN SEPTEMBER, 1858.—"Among the most precious instructions of my mother,—now fourteen years in Heaven!—were those that taught me reverence for the purity and loveliness of her sex, and that these demand my chivalrous protection to maintain them before the world. Fortunate, indeed, was I in having her so long before me as their representative, and my sacred ideal. In my social relations in life, any who seem less pure than she, fall at once below my standard."

In JANUARY, 1860.—Referring to his father's death, which occurred at that date, he wrote : "It is hard to believe that my father is gone. I do not think I shall ever again feel his loss as I did while he was living, after I left home and lost his daily companionship and counsels. I have slowly learned to live without them—and now, though I miss him, I can never experience such deep, unhealing grief as I have known for my precious mother."

II.

Early Manhood—Work "Within."

We have not wings, we cannot soar,
  But we have feet to scale and climb
By slow degrees, by more and more
  The cloudy summits of our time.
            —Longfellow.

Your future does not depend, as some will tell you, upon circumstances ; upon the passing accidents of the hour ; nor does it depend upon the adversities, perplexities, and snares, which beset your path in life ; it depends on your own will ; on your own determination : on the aim and purpose in life which you have set yourself to : on the character of the foundations on which you are building ; and above all it depends on your christian faith.—*Hepworth.*

Samuel Warren Hall, the father of Henry, was a man of method and integrity. In his business as village merchant, he had little to occupy his sons in their school vacations, till they were old enough to assist in the sales. He realized the importance of fixing early habits of industry and thrift ; and with parental tenderness he united unyielding firmness on questions of duty. A neighbor who had noticed from time to time in his drives, the two brothers — Henry and George

(18)

—gathering stones into piles on a bit of pasture land belonging to their father, and then again removing them to make other piles, inquired of Mr. Hall why they were set about such useless and . stupid business.

"It is work," was the pleasant reply, "and any harmless work is better for boys than idleness."

Ready to supply them with every available facility for education, and often assisting their home researches from his own well-furnished mind, he wished his sons to grow into systematic, energetic, useful men ; and as soon as he was old enough to be trusted with responsibilities, Henry had occasional sessions of business routine under the parental eye. This was excellent training for the future man, but it wrought more than the designer intended, namely, his deliberate preference for mercantile life, when his friends were hoping to see him enter one of the professions.

Having accepted a clerkship, that soon grew into responsibilities of magnitude, he went in the autumn of 1849, to New York City. Among his private papers of that period he kept a body of resolutions endorsed on the back with the date of his departure from the Ashfield home, and "*Forever*" underneath in his clear, full hand-writing. These resolutions, too sacred for any human eye, were intended by him to cover all the possibilities of temptation to a young man, amid the fascinating snares of a great city. For more than a year he went in and out before his employers in a large mercantile house, and up and down the thoroughfares of duty or recreation, wrapped about, as he afterward said, "with this garment of self-righteousness." It was a perfect moral code. To a friend he wrote soon after his arrival :

"I have been here nine weeks. You can never know into what temptations a young man is thrown in such a city as this. The utmost bounds of my expectations when I came, are but centres of the 'limitless vast.' Crime stalks the streets of what is usually called civilized New York. In my own boarding house are persons into whose rooms I shall never pass—whose acquaintance I shall never cultivate—and this is a christian family. I say it frankly, though I say it in confidence, that I *determined* when I came here that I would live close to New England puritan principles. There I put down my stake —and *there I will abide.*

* * * * From my earliest youth, thanks to the teachings of my angel mother, it has been my daily practice to read a portion of God's word before I laid my head upon my pillow. This I still continue to do. I resolved when I came here that I would choose a place of weekly worship, and make that my Sabbath home. This I have already done."

His chosen "Sabbath home" was the Broad-way Tabernacle, and under the ministry of its young and gifted pastor, and in its young men's Bible-class under training of Deacon Pitts of sainted memory, he spent the mornings and the evenings of the Lord's day. There, week after week, he listened to truths that were arrows in the seams of his faultless "garment." Thus far he had kept himself unspotted from the world by daintily gathering up his principles from contact with evil—and by carrying upon his lips the "stand thou apart" of the Pharisee as his hourly watchword. Intellectually, he well knew his duty, and the clear conditions of a blessed and fruitful life; but his proud spirit had elected its office to claim the heavenly benediction by a fair record of negative virtues. He was living unto himself. His diary notes the dates of the sermons and the impressions he received from them.

"Neglect not the gift that is in thee."—"Take heed unto thyself, and the doctrine."—" Let no man despise thy youth, but be thou an example unto the believers in conversation, in charity, in faith, in purity."—" Even the spirit of truth whom the world cannot receive because it seeth Him not, neither knoweth Him, but ye know Him, for He dwelleth in you."—" Whosoever believeth in Him shall have eternal life."—"Without father, without mother, without descent, having neither beginning of days nor end of life; but made like unto the Son of God."—"Who is made not after the law of a carnal commandment, but after the power of an endless life."—"Therefore He is able to save them to the uttermost that come unto God by Him, who is holy, harmless, undefiled, separate from sinners."—"For in that He himself hath suffered, being tempted, He is able to succour them that are tempted." —"Thou shalt love the Lord thy God with all thy heart, and with all thy soul, and with all thy strength, and with all thy mind ; and thy neighbor as thyself."

These, and many more weapons of the Spirit, were silently doing their work. His mind, never yet satisfied, grew more and more troubled. One Sabbath evening in May, 1851, he took his accustomed seat in the sanctuary in deep spiritual darkness. Stripped and bare of his own theories, his quivering soul needed to be clothed upon. Mr. Thompson met him with the master's own persuasive invitation :

"Come unto me, all ye that are weary and heavy laden, and I will give you rest. Take my yoke upon you, and learn of me, —for my yoke is easy and my burden is light."

Melted by the pleading eloquence of the almost inspired preacher, and won to grateful adoration by the voice of the Lord who tenderly called, he then and there yield everything, *and came to Him.* It was no partial surrender. Thenceforth he evidently walked "by faith and not by sight," and was rapidly moulded more and more into the image of him who is the Way, the Truth, and the Life.

In May, 1851, he wrote to a friend :—"From other topics I turn with a pleasure I never felt before, to inform you of my hope and trust in Jesus : and of my resolve that my future life shall be spent in usefulness—in the performance of His will, whatever that may be. Considering the subject in the light of duty, I could see no other course for me than the one provided by God through Christ,—but in the light of privilege, I do feel willing to do anything, or to be anything He shall appoint, if I may live for His honor who gave His life for me, and who deserves *the whole devotion of my soul.* * * * * Temptations are trials, yes, great ones—but O ! what peace does it bring to the soul to rise above them ! I have had knowledge this week of the peace given to them that overcome. 'Redeemed through the blood of Christ' rings in my ears, as I sit here writing to you. What are we without *Him!* We are to give *the light we receive.* Our supplies must come from the treasure-house above. When shall I learn to trust and love as I ought ? Hitherto I have relied on my own efforts to lead a blameless life—and how miserably have I failed ! Pray for me, that I may become strong in the power of His might, 'who needeth not daily, as those high priests, to offer up sacrifices first for His own sins, and then for the people's ; for this He did once when He offered up Himself—who is consecrated forever more.' * * * * I value decision of character, but I think I err on that side. in my prejudices. If a person is displeasing to me, I am apt to reveal too much dislike I must strive to cultivate the middle ground of that 'charity that suffereth long and is kind'—'that vaunteth not itself.'"

DECEMBER, 1851.—In December of that year he wrote : "It may perhaps gladden your heart to learn that on the first Sabbath of November I united publicly with the church. It was a happy Sabbath to me. My mother's prayers were answered. Where, what should 1 have been except for her influence on my life ? How much depends upon early impressions. How this conviction deepens at every turn of the life-current. Had you or I, with our firmness of character, been trained in a religion of formalism, how hard it would be to remould or even to modify our views. Are we suitably grateful for our New England heritage ? * * * * I am sometimes tempted to believe that God has permitted formalism to prevail among fickle and stupid nations to keep them steadfast by a blind faith ; but the Church of Christ must be an *aggressive* church. The constraining love of Christ !—I have dwelt on that subject much to-day. Abstractly, what a wonder is human life,—how mysterious our birth—our existence—the interruption and disappearance at death ; but how far more wonderful the development through life of the *constraining love of Christ* upon every faculty of body and mind ! ' It hath not entered into the heart of man to conceive' the measure of its power and blessing. ' Godliness is better for the life that now is,'—and then at death we change not, although we do cross the dark, mysterious river, except that when over, we have entered the New Jerusalem, and are in the innumerable company of the redeemed. There we are to see Jesus, and commune with Him face to face —and we are to know the heroes of our earliest Bible stories— Jacob and Joseph—Moses, Samuel, David, and a host beside !— *our names written in Heaven !*"

A few extracts from his private memoranda and correspondence during these years will not only gratify personal friends, but some of them may also mark the sincerity of his new aspirations. Those who knew him remember how entirely his interest in others permeated his own daily living—so that the genial friend became a glowing embodiment of spiritual graces—and the fastidious exponent of human excellence received, as a baptism, the inspiration of the Divine example in all his financial, political or social affairs — until, at length, the life became an enthusiastic struggle for the well-being of any whom, by utmost exertion, he could reach in the dear Master's name.

FEBRUARY 21, 1853. * * * Saturday evenings are always given to our Bible class prayer meeting, a precious hour—so fitting as we enter the portals of the Sabbath that we thus unlink ourselves from our worldly affairs.—Monday evenings are spent at Association Rooms. Three to five hundred young men all working together harmoniously for one common object. This evening a native of Syria was proposed as a member, whose birthplace was hard by that of our Saviour in Bethlehem, and whose youth was spent amid scenes so sacred to every christian heart. At announcement of his name his dark features were lustrous with the higher aspirations as he extended his hand to us in the bonds of our common faith.

FEBRUARY 28, 1853. * * * I must go in five minutes to the annual meeting of our little Ragged School, near Five Points. I have been strongly urged to consider lucrative business openings in a western city—but I have only time now to tell you that I think I shall do well to consider the power of Christian influence at this stand point of our country. The severing of a commercial artery is felt everywhere—we need Christian merchants in New York. I firmly believe it is my duty to work here. In the sunlight of His presence I have enough whether I go here or there, or up on high to be with Him who is, and was, and is to be ! But each new acquirement here fits us for more exalted joys there, and there is no lack of opportunity for growth here—with all the work there is to be done.

ASHFIELD, JUNE, 1853.—Home, my own room. My heart has been bounding with joy this entire day. I am luxuriating among flowers, and breathing whole gales of perfume. Oh ! these breezes are life-giving after dusty New York. The birds have ceased their carols, but the crickets, with voices unchanged, are chirping the same note we heard when other faces smiled around us, and other voices echoed through this home. * * * My drive yesterday, through the suffocating dust of the train, was relieved by earnest conversation with a favorite teacher in Williston Seminary, for the last five years in Georgia. A gentle shower in this region prepared us for a delightful drive to Ashfield,—the hill-sides were dotted with laurels in full blossom—the atmosphere was full of sweet odors—and birds filled the air with melodies. * * * I have just killed a bat—slew him with " The Mysteries of Paris "—the only good service the book ever rendered. I wish ——— would select other books to read. 3

JUNE 25. * * * Met R. at door of Adams stage, who had received his first impressions of New England scenery through the mountain passes from Savoy. After tea, with strawberries and cream—that were never so many nor so delicious—we took a stroll up to our village 'lake,'—which R. might have named Loch Katrine—as the drive over the hills had revived memories of his native Highlands. Going beyond, we had a magnificent view of your "Switzerland." * * * Retiring early, we kneeled together for our devotions. Oh! how often, under this roof, has my sainted mother whispered the evening petitions over my head, with her good-night kiss and blessing!

Later.—A welcome thunder shower to help vegetation—a magnificent display of the power of God in the forces of nature! I write at midnight—all is silent around me—Ashfield, at this hour, is at peace. May the Great Keeper watch over all the sleeping ones in this dear home of my boy-hood.

JULY 25. * * * I send you Mr. Everett's speech. It is a noble effort. I am proud of my native State when I see her great men thus swaying the minds of the nation. * * * Last evening I had a long talk with dear old Mr. ———, strong temperance man, you know. Attended State Temperance Convention at Springfield—thinks the Maine Law is bound to triumph and "*revangelize the world.*"

NEW YORK, AUGUST, 1853. * * * Last evening, Dr. Murray (Kirwan) lectured to young men. "It is good for a man that he bear the yoke in his youth." Birth and circumstances have much to do with future development of character. Had an Egyptian instead of an Israelitish nurse been called for Moses, mark the probable future career of the "Man of God." Had Napoleon been a victim of superstition in childhood, who could estimate the results upon the kingdoms of his power? Apparent trifles fix character. Moral and intellectual power are to control in the present age. An appeal to train thoroughly the intellect and the heart, if young men would be a power in the world. Closed with an impressive application,—and then leaning over the desk, said, from the depths of his warm Irish heart, "God bless you, young men!" * * * * I suppose it is impossible to understand the full force of our reflective influence on the world around us. If the days of our years are three score and ten, we shall die too young in Christian graces.

AUGUST, 1853. * * * On Tuesday afternoons, the meetings of the Board of Com. are public, and the latest missionary news are communicated. Usually, one or more from our church attend, and, in the evening, report at our monthly concert. To-night, China was the country from which we gathered information. I have long thought the present rebellion in China is in the hands of God to effect a change by which that mighty Empire shall be opened to the messengers of Christ.

NOVEMBER 21, 1853. * * * I wish I could give you my ideal of a Christian merchant. I have longed, from my boyhood, for a training that would fit me for that sphere—and now that God, by His providence, has opened my life as an active business man, I hope I may not be less active in His service than if I had been hedged in by a profession. I believe a true Christian merchant, in his direct access to men of all classes and conditions, wields an influence second to none. Such an one, at death, leaves an impress on the world—and *living after death* is a deep and comprehensive reality.

NEW YORK, NOVEMBER 25, 1853.—It is said that the legislature will be thoroughly "temperance," and that *the Maine Law will pass.* This is matter for rejoicing, though I am not prepared to say I wish to see it pass in this State, with all its provisions. Though just the thing for Maine, the same prescription cannot be applied to all forms of the same disease. Public morals and public opinion here must be elevated before such a law can be supported in this city. However, under our new reform charter, we are hoping better things. I am in favor of enacting the most stringent law it is possible to enforce—but I hold that a law *un*-obeyed is worse than *no* law. *Principle is sacred*—but opinions and preferences may be compromised, and often with profit to character.

MARCH, 1854. * * * "One country, one constitution, one destiny," said Mr. Webster in '37, and again published, it passed under my eye a moment since. I was thinking how the raging elements of sectional strife have been stirred during the two months past. I *did* hope the compromise of '50 would soothe all these passions. Such master spirits as took the helm, and guided the ship through that struggle are not now to be heard above the roar of the waves. * * * The sky looks dark, and I fear the North and the South are to array themselves in opposition. I do not think it is possible for the Nebraska Bill to pass the House as it is—the whole North are against it, and the South never have asked it. In short, it is the free-will offering of our Nadab, and the President has the audacity to support the character of Abihu in the same service. He may find that not all the people are called to perform the particular service of the sons of Levi * * * Their ambition has over-topped their wisdom, and their doom is irretrievably written.

APRIL 3, 1854. * * * Well, the Nebraska Bill died an easy death. Mr. C. performed his duty in a masterly manner even to the last. The defeat of the bill is a tremendous thrust at the administration.

APRIL 6, 1854. * * * More than a quarter century old ! With to-day pass twenty-six years of my life. These recurring birth-days are like mountain-tops, each succeeding one rising above the last, that I may overlook them all, with the shallow valleys between. To-morrow I speed on again—with vision undimned—for it is only morning, verging toward noon. Looking over the past hill-tops to my early boy-hood, I see myself riding with my mother, just turning the brow of the hill above my grandfather's house—how many anniversaries have I since spent at that home, amidst the most joyful associations ! I remember the exact spot near "*the old bear tree.*" How many times have I run through that little belt of trees, lest I might encounter *another bear !* On the crest of that hill, at that hour, I became a responsible being. I cannot think how old I was. I only know I then and there thought the first thoughts I can call mine. With no memories before—what crowds of memories since !

MAY, 1854. * * * What a contrast yesterday's New York Sabbath to the quiet stillness of the day on the dear old Masschusetts hills. Prodigality and penury, virtue and vice, the lover of God and the lover of the world filling our streets—a mob and a row on City Hall steps—a suicide in Hoboken—

profligacy, drunkenness, profanity, and debasement—to meet the eyes of twenty-five thousand persons who, during the past week, have, for the first time, breathed *free air* and indulged in free thought in the harbor of New York. I am sure our streets were never, before yesterday, filled with such a mixed assemblage. Here the wealthy burgher of Hamburg, and there the cigar-vender of the Empire of the Sun,—the plebeian of the Alps side by side with the aristocratic Goth,—the sturdy yeoman of Denmark, the sanguine Hungarian, the waiting son of Poland,—all grades of German life mingling with Greeks, Turks, Italians, and wanderers from Tartary, Africa, and the Islands of the Seas—some from almost every nation and tribe and people.

We welcome them—who does not ? But with every such accession comes a new call for christian labor and faithful prayer. Nothing but christian faith and energy, such as exists in American puritan blood, can keep the true governing elements in proper hands. Native Americanism and christian love must be the ground work of our institutions. Otherwise, we fall. A fearful responsibility rests on every christian citizen within our borders.

JULY 22, 1854. * * * Mr. Thompson preached last Sabbath from the words, " Provide ye things honest as well in the sight of man, as in the sight of God,"—in view of the great financial events that have so moved New York during the months past. From Sunday School I went to the bedside of little Jamie, and after talking with him a while about Jesus, and praying at his request—for he said he felt better after I prayed with him before—I had a few words with his sorrowing mother, and left. On Thursday morning, passing up Broadway, I met the father and brother of Jamie, on their way down to tell me that during the previous night death had claimed his own,—and to request me to conduct the funeral service at 2 P. M., of that day. I could not refuse. These were the people who a few months before, refused with bitter maledictions even to receive a tract at my hands. I went, and I am sure the Saviour was with us.

OCTOBER 31, 1854. * * * Last week was somewhat barren of news. The great pulse of opinion was gathering power for the final expression. Elements are combining, and foul plans are concocting beneath the seemingly calm surface of society, which, in their development next week, will startle thousands who are not aware they are sleeping over bursting volcanoes. I hold now, as I have ever held, that it is the moral duty of every man in this Republic to watch the ballot-box as he would his purse : yes, to guard it with a keener scrutiny, since it is *his only guarantee of liberty.* Oh|! that the graves in New England would open—that those who sleep in them might re-inspirit some of her recreant children ! I thank God that I was born an American, and a son of Massachusetts.

NOVEMBER 1, 1854. — S —— and B ——. What faithful representatives of a free people ! Unable to furnish from our native-born citizens, men capable of serving as exponents of our system of government, we draw on Baden-Baden for representative to the Hague—and accept a refugee Frenchman as first choice for counselor at the almost defunct court of Castile ! And our administration is, if possible, more corrupt in its source, than weak in the appointment of its ministers.

DECEMBER 18, 1854. * * * Have been detained by appointment at Young Men's Christian Association Rooms, and must be brief. I wish you could look in upon one of these gatherings of the young men of New York. They are a precious company. To-night, solid figures were before us, giving statistics of crime and profligacy in this great city ; but appalling as they are, they give nothing like the reality. As I sat there, I heard a voice saying to each one of us, "My son, why stand ye here idle." Work among the abodes of poverty, filth, and degradation is not agreeable, even to the *least* fastidious taste —and I fear we are not ready to stoop to the fallen, as the Saviour did, that we may win them. *He laid His hands on them* in sympathy, and wept over their sins with great all-reaching sorrow. There was no patronage in His pity for the erring. He could be touched with the feeling of their infirmity, whatever it might be,—for "He was tempted *in all points* like as we are," while He was "providing" in his own earthly life and death, that stupendous plan of "escape."

JANUARY 8, 1855. * * * Against my inclinations, I have been elected President of our Missionary Association. I am strongly desirous of arousing more fully among our members, a missionary spirit. I want every young man to feel his *personal responsibility*, and act accordingly. Action without that feeling is spasmodic and unreliable, and often utterly fails when it is most needed, so *that* is the great point to be secured. Organizations may plan and accomplish great work for the world, but each individual man, unless heartily identified with some specific effort, loses his share of the privilege and blessing. We know that God will train up laborers for Himself, but shall we forfeit the birth-right and leave Him to give life to *stones*, that the work may be accomplished? * * * Mr. Thompson's sermon, last evening, from the words, "It is appointed unto men once to die," exhibiting the purposes of God as inevitable. In the application he appealed earnestly to young men, closing each appeal with, "but after death, the judgment."

FEBRUARY 17, 1855. * * * I am in my room this Saturday evening by reason of a rebellious foot, revenging the hardships of a heavy boot, or a boot too loose,—but I suffer most because I am deprived of my share in a delightful prayer meeting. I must rest to-night, so as to be in my place at church to-morrow. There is apparent interest in our church. A good work is manifest in our Bible class and *Mission School*. Down among the despised and wretched, many are sorrowing for their offences. Good, faithful Mr. Camp is receiving a part of his reward in this world. For nearly twenty years he has been toiling unremittingly in this hard field. Poor in purse, but rich in faith, he begins to reap though "the harvest is not till the end of the world." Surely, "they labor not in vain, who labor in the Lord."

To-day I bade good bye to Mr. M., a native of Odessa educated in this country and returning as a missionary to his own people. The storm prevented his ship from sailing till this morning. We parted at breakfast—he to go on board—I to go to my business—but to meet him at the dock at 12, M. On reaching the dock I found that the ship had hauled out into the stream. Took a boat and went off. No friend had said farewell to him, and he had given up America *alone*, when I surprised him on deck. I took his hand, and we went below, and had our parting in his state-room, kneeling together before the God of nations. Such interviews are few on earth. Now he sleeps on old ocean. May He, who holds the winds in His fist, protect him !

SEPTEMBER 10, 1855. * * * Business is good—but I wish we had the right sort of men in employ. There are men who can never deliver themselves of more than one idea per day, and probably that will come breadth-wise. * * * The greater struggle is, after all, not to amass wealth, but to act justly toward those who are placed as toward myself in subordinate capacities, and toward all the world as a christian gentleman. God only is our wisdom and our strength.

OCTOBER 12, 1855. * * * Dr. Kane is in New York again. Our papers are full of his wonderful trials, escapes, and discoveries. At a time when a political war is swaying the masses —when our city is stirred by the corruption and venality of its rulers, and the public mind is perplexed to know which is the wiser course to adopt, this interruption by the arrival of an honored explorer, almost given up for dead, with his thrilling tale from unknown lands, is an immense relief. The daily papers follow the journal of Dr. Kane with detailed accounts of the storming and overthrow of Sevastapol. Which is the true general—Kane, or Pellisier, or Simpson ? * * * At Mission Sabbath School I have my old class of boys, and took up the lesson where we left it in June. Upon the review they seem to have the whole ground distinctly before them, which gratifies and encourages me. I was touched by the salutation to-day of one dear little fellow,—"Oh, we've been so *lonesome* since you've been gone." The field is the world—but it does seem to me that one of these little ones redeemed from the very borders of the pit, is a double work of grace. Lessons over, I finished my monthly tract distribution in the Five Points district—and saw proofs that past labors have not been in vain. Sought out again, among others, the poor widow, whose case was so sad when I first found her. She sees light now, and her heart overflows with thanksgiving. Evening discourse on the morals of business and their relations to business men, was full of profit.

OCTOBER 15, 1855. * * * Came home early this evening, and after my private devotions, took my hat and went down through the Five Points to the chamber of the lone widow, whose case I mentioned yesterday. Found her still watching over the child, whose little life was almost spent. I pointed her to Him who gives and takes away. Then I offered prayer, the mother and little daughter, six years old, kneeling beside the cradle. They repeated with me the Lord's prayer, and I continued for a few moments in supplication to the widow's God. Doubtless the first protestant prayer, and perhaps the last, ever uttered under her roof. We wait for the judgment. When I left she lighted me down the rickety stairs with many thanks, and with quivering lips.

III.

Domestic and Social Life.

"His love was manly, and ennobled himself as well as its object. It was no whining, whimpering love, that thrives in moony nights, and talks of stars, or shivers over grates in winter, and dreams of summer coming again. It was no ball-room love, that lives in the touch of a gloved finger in a cotillion ; no such love as the men and the women of this day think and talk of. * * * They never exchanged an unkind word. From childhood to the end they placed unbounded confidence in each other. I believe if he had told her it was snowing on a hot August day, she would have put on a cloak to go out, and shivered at that,—so firm was her faith in all he said. He never had deceived her in thought or deed."

"Go, if you please
To the 'house-hold room' cushions, for comfort and ease—
            * * * The sanctum of bliss,
That holds all the comforts I least like to miss—
Where, like ants in a hillock, we run in and out ;
Where sticks grace the corners, and hats lie about ;
Where no idlers dare come to annoy or amuse
With their 'morning-call' budget of scandalous news ;
—Where I lounge in the 'house-hold room' taking my rest,
With a tinge on my cheek, and content in my breast."
                —*Eliza Cook.*

In June, 1855, Mr. Hall married his early choice, and established his domestic fireside, — first and second at boardings in University Place and Twentieth Street — then in the rented brown

(34)

stone cottage in Forty-Seventh Street — and finally in the Forty-Third Street *home.*

The memories of his relations with those whom he called "the precious quartette who are my very own," are now as ointment to a bruised heart — too sacred to be broken beyond the immediate circle who have a right to share them ; but this attempt to give his example to others would be sadly incomplete without allusions to his life as a father with his children, and as a host with his friends.

His pride and joy in his three sons were fruitful in all tender and wise ministries. Nothing within his power to command was withheld or overlooked, that could increase their true happiness, or enlarge their horizon. From their infancy, the deepest cry of his soul had been, "Lord, keep them from the evil ; " and as soon as they could discriminate between right and wrong he began to fortify them against the evil that so surely threatens every undeveloped mind. This evil was not to him a vague and shadowy theory, spinning itself into a web of wordy croakings in general, over "the wickedness of the world " — a flimsy web, that the first temptation might penetrate and overcome. He sought, first of all, to establish in their tender hearts strict loyalty and obedience to the Divine and the parental law *through love*, and not through fear. With this foundation he easily secured implicit confidence and trust, which as toward the Heavenly and the earthly Father was like that of friend to friend, — and then taking them by the hand from day to day, when life opened new snares and struggles to their little feet, he was ready with a quick, sharp watch-word for every point of defence.

It was his custom to call sins by their right names, that there might be *no mistaking the danger*. He believed his children were sent into the world to battle with evils, and he accepted his trust as guardian of their weak beginnings, with a vigilance that knew no abatement.

In all their plays he was a boy with them — and "the children's hour" in the Forty-Third Street library was a good-night round of uproarious mirth. They never missed the stroke of the clock, by a minute, for they well knew how grand were the frolics in store for them. The same hour on Sabbath evenings was spent in quiet talks about the infancy and childhood of Jesus — or in reviewing the narratives or biographies of Old Testament history. His Bible-story-telling had a perpetual charm, not only to the children, but to all the household. Those who have been guests in the family will not forget how surely they were attracted from social interests in any other part of the house, to the circle around the library grate — where, with one boy on his knee, and the other two leaning on his chair in rapt attention, he put into vivid but simple Saxon the outlines and the coloring of Scripture scenes and characters, till they were an indelible reality to his audience.

A gentleman asked one of these children, not five years old, whom he should wish most to see in the heavenly home: "I think I should find Mr. Noah first, because he can give me the exact dimensions of the Ark," was the prompt reply to the amazed and disappointed friend.

As they expanded into most natural and irrepressible desire for recreations outside their home, the delicate and generous distinctions made for them by the father only cemented the bond of their mutual sympathies. His own æsthetic tastes, and especially his passionate love for music of high order, prepared him to grant wise margins, while he held tightly the silken fetters of restraint. He made plain his choice of public amusements — regarding them as frivolous, dissipating, and sadly demoralizing snares, when indiscriminately indulged ; but he honored the talent of artists — even in opera, and in theatre — who seek to dignify themselves and to elevate the taste of patrons while gaining honorable support through the gifts they have received. When Ristori came to New York, he took his seat in the French Theatre with sincere regard for her as a woman, mingled with admiration for her as an actor.

A valued friend, whose life had been marked with peculiar blessing to society and the church — who could well afford, in purse as in conscience, to garland his palatial home at outlay of hundreds for a family fête or a bridal — met him soon after this occasion with serious admonition ; and in all sincerity asked a member of his family : "Did you find yourself in a prayerful state of mind before the play began ?" "Yes, I think I could truly give thanks for such a genius as Ristori." "Could you have read your Bible between the acts ?" "Yes, I *could* have read it, but I considered it more appropriate to read over the play." Then turn-

ing to Mr. Hall, "Would you take your children to such a place?" "Yes—*emphatically yes*
—to hear Ristori, or Booth, or any other exalted
exponent of histrionic art—*because* I hold that
both opera and drama will sooner or later allure
young people. If we forbid these pleasures they
will seek them by stealth, or bide their time
till they are their own masters,—but if I go
with my children to recognize and enjoy the
highest order of talent, they will thus establish
their standard, and will not only escape, but
avoid all that lies below it, with the attendant
dissipations."

The event proved the wisdom of his decisions.
The man who could stay three months in Paris,
without once seeing the fountains play in the
grounds of the Palace at Versailles, *because they
play only on Sundays*, when the excursion trains
to that suburb of the gay capitol were crowded,
week after week, with an eager throng of native
and foreign sight-seers, including many Americans who justified the indulgence of their curiosity on the ground that their example abroad
could not lead others astray—did not hesitate
to take his family to the theatre and the opera
in New York, on the very rare occasions, when

by going they might be helped and elevated. The one indulgence was *to him* plainly wrong — the other he considered plainly right — and he believed in doing openly, *and at home,* what he was willing to do at all.

His frequent absences from home and country gave his sons the rich legacy of his correspondence, and from these letters a few extracts are taken :

PULASKI HOUSE, SAVANNAH, GA., MARCH 21, 1865.—A great many hundred years ago, you recollect, there were three brothers, Shem, Ham, and Japheth. After the Ark rested on Mt. Ararat—you know where that is, on the map,—and the water had dried up, Ham took his wife, and I suppose the two camels, and after bidding good-bye to his father and mother, started off down through the country afterward occupied by the children of Israel, and where Jerusalem, and Nazareth, and Bethlehem, now are—down over the desert that you and I went over from Cairo, when we went to the Red Sea—over the river Nile—then away down across the great desert of Sahara, in Africa, and in the fruitful country below, lived on bananas, oranges, and figs.

Bye and bye, after centuries had passed away, Ham's great-great-grand-children, though many generations, were scattered all over Africa. One day, a tribe living near the coast quarreled with another tribe, and one took prisoners from the other. Just then, a little vessel from England was in one of the ports, loading up elephants' tusks, etc., and the white people on board bought these prisoners, and brought them to this port of our country, where I am now staying—and sold them to the farmers here, who made them work without pay. These farmers soon found that they could make money by having workmen without wages. So they sent to Africa for more,—till there were in this part of the country more than 4,000,000 of them—

more than four times as many men, women, and children, as there are living in New York. This is a short history of African slavery for you. * * *

Washington, D. C., February 13, 1866.—This morning I spent in the Patent Office. In one of the cases in the Great Hall is kept the original constitution of the United States. The *real* one, signed by John Hancock, Benjamin Franklin, and all the other noble men, who knew at the moment they signed their names, that if the English army could catch them they would cut off their heads,—the same constitution that your Uncle N—— and five hundred thousand more brave men died to protect ; the same that I am sure my own little boys will always be most watchful to guard, even with their heart's blood, if that be necessary. * * *

Nantucket, August 7, 1867. * * * Passing a night at Hyannis we took carriage next morning and drove to Yarmouth, to ascertain more about your ancestors who lived and died there,—whose memory I hope you will always cherish, not only because they were worthy and honorable men, but because they loved their country better than they loved their lives. In an old book we saw the registry of one who was an officer in King Phillip's war—and later, numbers of them were active in the war of the Revolution. I had a long talk with the ancestral Halls, among whom, in my direct line, there has not been wanting a living ' deacon ' through a period of more than two hundred years. The old school mstaer Hemphill, in writing to Increase Mather, says, "the original John Hall and all his family are eminently faithful and consistent Christians." Mr. Otis says, "through more than two centuries the Halls have not been so much noted in politics as in their devotion to everything valuable in morals and religion."

I slept last night near the ancient grave-yard at Yarmouth— where the Halls lie buried. Have trodden soil, and passed dwellings made better through the sweat of their brows,—and hope I have gained something from this visit to the *old Sod.*

New York, April 28, 1868. * * * Your nice letter was forwarded to me in Washington, where I was witnessing the progress of President Johnson's trial for violating his oath to uphold the constitution of the United States. You know we

Americans consider *that* to our national life what the Bible is to
our spiritual life. I shall never forget the scene. The wisdom
and the talent of a nation deliberating, with God's oath upon
them, over the sad errors of its chief magistrate. Never
before has such a trial taken place in this country, and I trust
that you, and the thousands of other boys who are to take the
places of those who now rule, will be so vigilant to preserve
the constitution that such a spectacle will never be witnessed
here again.

NANTUCKET, SEPTEMBER, 1868. * * * A few days ago a
whale ship came in here ; an event which seldom happens now-
a-days. We were at dock when she hove to,—and after she
'made fast.' I went on board to see how she looked after being
at sea eighteen months. Now I have an example in arithmetic
for you ! The ship brought 400 barrels of sperm oil, which is
sold at $1.85½ per gallon. There are twelve sailors, one second
mate, one first mate, and a captain. Each sailor has one-for-
tieth the price of the oil ; the second mate *twice* as much ; the
first mate *three times* as much ; the captain twice as much as
the first mate. The balance goes to the owners of the ship.
How much does each get ? * * *

EAST WHATELY, DECEMBER 28, 1869.—(Writing to the two elder
sons, who had been placed in a family school.)—Three young
gentlemen, named Papa, W., and H., propose to read each day
during the year 1870, commencing January 1st, one chapter in
the Bible—taking the following in course, viz : Genesis, 50—
Proverbs, 31—Eccl., 12—Daniel, 12—New Testament, 265. No
one allowed to read one day for any other day. The oldest of
the three young gentlemen will pay two dollars to either of the
younger who makes the fewest failures in daily reading. Who
wins ? Answer to be given January 1st, 1871.

MONTREAL, MAY 5. * * * When you are old enough
to realize how invaluable are a strong, active brain and mind
in a sound body, you will be more than ever grateful to the
friends who are caring for you. See how much you can do
for them and for others in the world ; for after all, the great
secret of living, of *true* living, has not changed a particle in two
thousand years. 'Doing for others' was the teaching of a very
obscure man then, in opposition to 'getting for self' as taught

by the great and learned of that time.   Who is conqueror to-
day ? * * *

LAGO MAGGIORE, HOTEL DES ISLES BORROMEES, STRESA, ITALY,
JUNE 7, 1869.—Dear H. and G. : Last Saturday morning we left
Milan, once the capital of Piedmont and Lombardy,—you will
easily find it on the map,, in the northern part of Italy,—and
came by rail to Arona at the foot of this lake, which our In-
dians would call Big Lake instead of Lake Maggiore, as it means
the same.   In coming here we passed over several of the battle
fields of ancient history.   In one pláce where Hannibal fought
a great battle with the Romans—not your favorite elephant .at
Barnum's, but *General* Hannibal, who came from Africa to
conquer the country, and used elephants to carry his guns and
camp equipage.   Even now the bones of some of them are
found here.   From Arona we came for an hour and a half along
the lake to the hotel which overlooks it.   Our rooms were just
vacated by the King of Prussia, who had come here to see this
beautiful portion of Italy.   You have read about the Italian
Lakes, and have seen pictures of them, but never can any
words or pictures convey the loveliness of them all.

Around the margin of this lake, as far as we can see, are
cozily-stowed-away-villages, with here and there a castle
crowning a point.   Just back of these are high mountains, and
back of them higher mountains, and back of these still higher
mountains, and yet beyond, the great snow-covered Alps that
have never been reached by the foot of man.   In the lake are
islands studded with cottages, and on one of them is the summer palace of a Duke, fitted up at an outlay of millions, with
statues and hanging-gardens, so that it appears to be floating
in the air.

Here, under the shadow of these mountains among which,
in some places, it is sunset at ten o'clock in the morning, we
passed the Sabbath. * * * In front of this hotel passes the
great road built by the First Napoleon, just after he had crossed
with his armies over the Alps, almost without roads, to win the
battle of Marengo.   After the victory he told his engineers to
bring him surveys and plans for a smooth, safe road from
France to Italy.   At that time this was a greater undertaking
than the Pacific Rail Road now is.   When he had selected the

plan he liked best, he said, "Go on ! How soon can I bring cannon over the Simplon ?" Then thirty thousand men worked six years till the road was completed : and though seventy years have since passed, it is now a superb highway, as smooth and as wide as the drives in Central Park, built along mountainsides where birds could not have found footing, and under and over cataracts higher than a half-dozen Niagaras. Last evening, as the shadows were gathering on the high mountain-tops, I went out and sat in a quiet place where the lake—with the great mountains reflected in its sweet waters—lay at my feet, and this road at my side,—and thought of this greatest of European monarchs, and of his tremendous sway while he lived. For months, we had been travelling where his power had been felt as a conqueror, and I now sat by this great highway over which nations could interchange thought and substance—which, next to God's word, civilize man most rapidly. I thought of his power and greatness—and then I thought of Him who, eighteen hundred years before, opened the strait and narrow way over the mountains of man's transgressions. In one or two centuries this high-way will be surpassed by something better—and the name of Napoleon will be forgotten. But centuries after these wild mountains are destroyed, the name of Him who is the Way, the Truth, and the Life, will be remembered and magnified by ten thousand times ten thousand, and thousands of thousands.

The Blessed Jesus keep you in "the narrow way."

Lovingly, your Papa.

DECEMBER 28, 1869. * * * Your Saviour has left a special blessing for those who commence *early* to do right. If you seek instruction through prayer, you will never wander so far from the truth as to be unable to return. *Pray a great deal.* When you are doubtful which is the right way, ask Jesus. When boys and men tempt you to do wrong, *as they surely will,* ask Jesus not only to help you, but to change the hearts of those who tempt you. I would not be guilty of giving Him half a heart. * * * That you may be steadfast, immovable, always abounding in a good, pure, and blessed life, is the constant prayer of your loving father.

NEW YORK. DECEMBER 11, 1871. * * * Do not be small or

mean in the use of money. Be prudent, but at the same time
be generous and manly, *always doing your part handsomely,*
whatever that may be. * * *   .

PARIS, AUGUST, 1868. * * * I have written you of the
Alps and of Geneva, which we left nearly four weeks ago. W.
accompanied us the entire length of the lake, and visited By-
ron's Castle of Chillon, where Bonivard was seven years con-
fined in a dungeon, because he loved the Saviour. When he
was set free by the Swiss troops, Geneva was a republic, and
openly professing the reformed faith. Returning, W. went
back to Geneva alone—brave boy—and we left the steamer at
Lausanne, because we wanted to see the place where Gibbon
wrote his History of Rome,—and more because we wanted to
see Madames H—— and B—— who have done so much to
help poor Spanish christians. * * *   From Lausanne we
went by rail to Berne, which means Bear,—named so, because
a man who built a house there killed a bear near his door—
and now the people of that city are very fond of bears. They
have a den filled with them, kept at the public expense, and
they have the city filled with them in stone carvings, that are
not *now* expensive to anybody. Besides all the stone bears on
the fountains, and signs, and at the street corners, there are
some wooden bears that shew themselves every day in a
curious clock outside an old prison-tower, which is now a gate-
way. One minute before the hour strikes, a cock comes out,
flaps his wings, crows twice, and goes back,—then the figure of
a man on the top of the tower strikes the hour with a hammer
on a bell—next, a long procession of *bears* come out, and pass
before a figure on a throne, who marks the hour by gaping,
turning over the hour-glass he holds in one hand, and lowering
the sceptre he holds in the other. In the Museum, is the
stuffed skin of "Barry" the famous and noble St. Bernard dog,
who saved so many lives in the Alps. My next letter will tell
you about the Alpine Glaciers.

His playfulness gave sparkle and zest to the
social atmosphere around him. No one more
keenly enjoyed a harmless joke, when practiced

on himself, and his return aim was always that
of a skillful shot.   He held the confidences of
a multitude of young people, and used often to
say he hoped he should never be insane, for in
that case he "might betray a conglomerate of
trusts, and mix up things dreadfully."

Young men in the city found in him a safe
advisor and a genuine friend.   Remembering with
impressions that could only take lasting shape in
a nature of sensitive mould, how really alone
he felt when, a boy of twenty-one, he began
his life work in a crowded city, he never lost
opportunity to support strangers who came to
the same heart-wearying field.   Long after his
limit of age expired, he continued his connexion
with the Sunday morning Bible class in the social rooms of the new Tabernacle, not only that
he might invite strangers to its safe environment,
but that he might extend their acquaintance
among its members.

He cultivated a perpetual interest in the welfare of the homeless.   They were frequently
invited to his own home which he illumined
with rare hospitalities.   Many of them had standing offer of seats at his table, or in the family
pew.   On occasion of festivals, especially the

New England Thanksgiving-day feast, his enjoyment of family reunions was tempered by thoughts of those who were sitting apart from their kindred over the scanty delights of boarding-house fare. Often, one or more of these would receive welcome to his elected circle, and on one Thanksgiving day he satisfied his generous heart by entertaining a house full of students and clerks, giving them, as he said, "a good New England dinner in the name of their mothers at home."

Students of theology came to him with their problems and plans. Many are now in the ministry who can recall his open-handed encouragement when they were struggling through the mysteries of demand and supply — for though he never talked of these attentions to others, he was a man of exactness *to a penny* in the entry on his private memoranda of all expenses, among which some of this character are now a valued souvenir. They were often at his fire-side. To those who were primed for experimental parish work he had a harvest always ready in the mission schools and rounds of visitation in upper New York.

Into one of these schools, as Superintendent, he projected the spirit that thoroughly possessed

him, so that when his health failed, and other
earnest men took up the privilege, he still continued a frequent and welcome visitor, staying
the hands, and encouraging the hearts of his
successors by his own strong faith. The grand
corps of christian men who now sustain the out-
growths of that mission by their large financial
pledges, and by their constant prayers and labors,
may better than any others speak of the personal magnetism and of the unfailing courage
which they miss.

The sons of the church, whose aims were
higher than their means, never looked to him
in vain for influence to secure material aid from
the noble company of those whom he affectionately called "brother"—and to whom God had
given wealth, with hearts to dispense it liberally.
He used to say "the final records alone will
reveal what they have done, and are doing to
bless New York and the world." The observation is here repeated as a tribute from his
heart to theirs. Each knows his name, and his
place in the abiding confidence and love of the
"brother" gone.

During a critical relapse in his last illness,
one of these "brothers" was prostrated by a

rapidly consuming fever. The physician of the one was the physician of the other, and "brother" to both. In the sick chamber of each the Angel of Death seemed only waiting. The life of the long suffering invalid seemed to himself of less account than the life of his friend. He watched eagerly for the almost hourly bulletins recorded for his relief. Brief, but searching questions probed the veil of calmness with which the beloved messenger of healing went to and fro. He spent much time in prayer. The church also was crying aloud. The young men gathered in groups from day to day, in the intervals of business, and besought the Great Physician to restore these friends. Toward daylight, on the fifth morning, after a night of special pleading, Mr. Hall opened his eyes with peculiar gladness and exclaimed, with a smile breaking over his pale face, "Prayer is answered ! Mr. B —— will live ! How much he can do in the world with his wealth, and with his earnest heart. If I should stay, I could never be strong again. It is better for him to stay, and for me to go." The assurance came only to *him* for many days, but from that hour he never doubted the result.

His religious sentiments only softened while they heightened the glow of his social presence. Those who entered the private circle where he was best known and admired, were won, almost imperceptibly, to a life that brought such overflow of joy and peace — such exuberant gladness to him who possessed it.

His principles permeated with all simplicity and candor his social, domestic, and financial affairs. The Divine indwelling was apparent in the magnetic grasp of his hand, and in the pure, clear light of his loving eyes, — but there was never a breath of *cant* in the tones of his voice, nor in his far-reaching aims for "good will to men." He believed there are good men and good women engaged in *all* beneficent enterprises — and he respected all endeavors, of whatever name, undertaken to elevate society and the world. "They are all doing their best according to the light they have," he used often to say, while at the same moment his very soul was stirred in efforts to concentrate *more light.* The light that was in him was the clear, unclouded sunlight of inspiration, — and though not as a bigot, nor as a hard-grained Calvinist, yet as a grateful, willing subject, — as a trusting

child, — he held unwavering faith in a Triune
God. The doctrines of evangelical faith were
factors of the great whole accepted by his logi-
cal mind under the revealed relations between
the Creator and the created, — and not as the
partial edicts of a cruel Sovereign. *The fore-
knowledge* of events, as a necessary attribute of
omniscience; *free-agency*, by belief that the
human nature given by the all-loving Father
through Eden to the world, was created sinless,
and with perfect poise between good and evil;
original sin, by sacred history not only, but by
daily evidence in his own life and in other lives,
that when put to the test, the balance turned
toward evil *by voluntary choice of the created*,
and that thus man's nature became sinful.
Then, the stupendous scheme of restoration by
sacrifice — typical in the Old Testament — expia-
tory in the New, — through which were developed the majesty and the condescension, and the
compassion of God; and these revealed to man
from first to last, — from the scene in Eden to
the scene in Gethsemane, — in the triple attri-
butes of Creator, Redeemer, and Comforter.
One God in three by justice, by mercy, and by
peace to fallen man; but *three in one* by unity

of power, plan, and result from the foundation
of the world.

How clear and simple were his statements of
his faith to others! And to minds perplexed
concerning the great mystery of the Divine nature investing the human, and the offices of the
Holy Spirit in the soul, he would bring proofs
from the Divine Word itself so plainly shining
with this light that "he who runs may read"
— or, quoting from some favorite uninspired
testimony, of which his mind was full — as this
from Whittier :

"* * * Revealed in love and sacrifice,
  The Holiest passed before thine eyes,
One and the same, in three-fold guise ;
  The equal Father in rain and sun.
His Christ, in the good to evil done—
  His voice, in thy soul—and the Three are One."

Or, this from Bushnell, whose writings were
a great delight to him :

"The world has never been the same since Jesus left it. The
air is charged with heavenly odors ; and a kind of celestial con-
sciousness, a sense of other worlds, is wafted on us in its breath.
It were easier to untwist all the beams of light in the sky, sepa-
rating and expunging one of the colors, than to get the character
of Jesus, which is the real Gospel, out of the world. * * *
Do you require us to show you who He is, and definitely to ex-
pound His person ? We may not be able. Enough to know
that He is not of us,—some strange being out of nature and
above it *Whose name is Wonderful.* * * * 'Behold the Lamb
of God that taketh away the sins of the world !'"

Further quotations from his letters will show how, at the same time, his outward life was going on through the quiet under-current of generous activities. In the financial crisis of '56 to '58, he did not escape anxieties, which at times amounted to serious apprehensions ; but with all his cares in the counting-room, he found time for his higher duties.

JULY, 1856.—I trust there is not to be calamity, but should such pressure continue, no house could live. If we are robbed of wealth, the advantages that flow from dispensing to others will be withdrawn, but we cannot be robbed of our greatest riches, and I have been strangely calm and happy through it all. Have just returned weary from our Tabernacle prayer-meeting. My heart is filled with peace and gratitude. How do those live who never pray ? * * * As I opened my Bible last night my eye rested on these words, " Call upon me in the day of trouble : I will deliver thee, and thou shalt glorify me." *I believed it.* The hour of prayer that followed was precious to my soul.

SABBATH, P. M., JULY, 1856. * * * I always feel a want when I rise from an unblessed table, which I did to-day—but the blessing came with Dr. Thompson's morning sermon from Luke 10:20. *Our names written in Heaven !* * * * Visited through my Five Points' tract district this p. m., and went to my class in Mr. Camp's Mission Chapel. Bartie was there punctually. The dear little fellow improves in reading. *That Bible* is his daily food. As I talked and read with the class concerning the rich man and Lazarus, his eyes were fixed upon me, most intently, as if to learn the whole. He has a giant heart in his poor crippled body. He still gathers bottles.

JULY, 1856. * * * Had a capital tea to-night.—bread and butter with kindness ; other relishes with social sauce. Discussed the funniest and latest excitement, viz : the great hullabaloo English papers are making because an American army officer happened to offer himself at court in a white instead of a black cravat. The Times, the horns of Johnnie Bull, cries out, "when will Americans learn manners?" It would have been better, surely, had the gentleman conformed to court requirements, or remained away—but the bullying Times-man would have displayed himself less a fool and more a man, had he bestrode a gentler beast.

You know two men once went up to pray—and the crying sin of one was that he thanked God he was not like other men. The question has arisen whether I might not expose myself to equal guilt, if I were to express here all my sentiments.

AUGUST, 1856. * * * Of the three presidential candidates I prefer Fillmore. He is a Whig, a sound, safe, tested man—not a great statesman, nor holding extraordinary powers of mind, but a man of sound common sense, which he has exercised in calling around him as counsellors, the most eminent men of the nation. He has also proved it in his readiness to acknowledge the success of his administration, not because he is President, but because he had so able advisors. But I doubt if Fillmore can be elected.

SEPTEMBER, 1856. * * * Mr. Thompson preached this A. M. from the words, "The law is holy and the commandment holy, and just and good." The discourse was received with marked attention by a full audience. * * * The amassing of gold will not satisfy me—something higher, nobler, must be my study. If God gives me wealth it must be a means to an end—even for His glory who has redeemed me by the blood of Christ.

Evening. Went to Dr. Cheever's church to hear Dr. Taylor of New Haven. Just as he arose for prayer, the gas went out. He waited a moment in silence, and then began—"O Thou who dwellest in light unapproachable," etc.

SABBATH, SEPTEMBER, 1856. * * * Went this morning to Missionary Association Rooms. Then Mr. Thompson preached from the words, "Peter, Satan desires to sift you as wheat, but I have prayed for you that you may be delivered from temptation." He dwelt upon the love of Jesus, who prayed for poor

Peter, even when he saw that temptations were to overwhelm him with shame and grief. The love of Christ! who shall fathom it!

PRINCETON, MASS., NOVEMBER, 1857.—Arrived here last evening. Sermon to day from the text, "Faint, yet pursuing." Appropriate to the times. Bad as is the financial position in New York, there are thousands along this valley from Providence to Princeton that are bankrupt to-day. Not the sound of a spindle, wheel, hammer, nor shuttle, as I passed by the factories yesterday. As though a plague had passed over these villages, all was hushed. "Hard times" the absorbing topic among employers, and among the employed the great underwail of approaching want. Where will be the end?

JULY, 1858. * * * I have had faith to believe that we shall be led into open day. Yet I find myself, like Christian in Bunyan, doubting and questioning, fearing lest we may be led *into the vortex.* Oh how unlike the promises of men are those that come from Galilee and the region round about Jordan! My heart does sometimes overflow with rapturous desire to overleap the confines of its earthly career, and to commence its freely given life at the feet of Jesus.

CLINTON, MASS., JULY, 1858. * * * Reached Worcester weary, but after a half hour's sleep felt much refreshed, and after reading Choate's 5th July address, felt ready for anything. I beg you to improve your first leisure in reading it carefully. Study it—think over it—and let its ruling principles and great thoughts be instilled into W——s mind as he advances. It has been many years since I have read anything so fully expressing in its general features my views of the only true platform on which an American should stand. One is carried back to the days of Clay and Webster.

SEPTEMBER, 1858. * * * These eight or nine years of my city life have brought with them lessons. Some have been learned under the lash: all have been for reproof, for correction, or for instruction in righteousness. I have sometimes thought how glad I should be if W—— could enter upon life with something like a rational idea of the world in which he is to live and act. But then I remember that children could not

be pure and guileless if they inherited the experiences of those
who lead them. We should study to know more of the truth,
and the perfect way, so to lead him, that he may become strong
in the Lord, and able to resist the infirmities of men.

October 3, 1858. * * * Have dwelt to-day upon the duties
and privileges of God's people, with especial reference to increased activity in our own church. More personal effort—
more vigorous action, in Sabbath school—in Bible-class— in
prayer meetings— every where and always intent upon the one
great end. This sowing the seed by all waters, who can measure the result ? He only who has said, " Ye labor not in vain
in the Lord."

IV.

Work "Without."

There is no man's calling doth so confine him, but were his heart and his affections heavenly and spiritual, his thoughts would force passage through the crowd of worldly business to Heaven. Ejaculations are swift messengers—they need not much time to deliver their errand, or much time to return again to the soul. You may point your earthly employments with heavenly meditations, as men do their writing with stops, ever now and then sending up a thought into Heaven ; and such pauses are no hindrance to your earthly affairs.

—*Bishop Hopkins.*

It is fortunately part of the immortality of human goodness that it leaves a perpetual benediction upon the places that knew it, so that they acquire a deeper beauty, and a subtler charm.—*George Wm. Curtis.*

In October, 1860, Mr. Hall went to Southern Spain with an invalid member of his family. Reaching London, he soon found his way to Paternoster Row, where he selected large packages of tracts and "portions," especially the Gospels, printed in the Spanish language. While paying for them, the attendant said, "Allow me to ask you, sir, if these are designed for distribution in Spain?" adding, "do you know it is

4

as much as your life is worth to undertake this work?" The one standing by his side saw a great light playing over his face, as he cheerily answered, "it is the message of Him who holds my life in His hands. I am not afraid to carry it."

No sign of fear was ever made in all that journey, though he went through the length and breadth of the peninsula *with a price on his head*. From the day he entered Malaga harbor till he crossed by diligence the northern pass of the Pyrenees at Irun, — from Barcelona to Madrid, — from Cadiz to Burgos — he scattered crumbs of truth broadcast, tucking a tract or a "portion" into the pocket of a diligence here — or slipping a leaflet into the crevice of a posada-wall there, — or distributing discreetly among the brethren whom, by some keen spiritual recognition, he found almost everywhere. He had not been many days in Malaga before the secret pass-word had been exchanged. Those who had found light held all their re-unions at midnight, for fear of the priests. One by one they were accustomed to glide along the city streets till they reached the place of rendezvous, dropping in at intervals from front and rear, to avoid the vigilence of the police. Those midnight meetings he frequently attended, when from the leaflets he brought openly through the customs — but which were passed unseen — they sang the hymns so dear to many hearts: "There is a fountain filled with blood," — "Just as I am without one plea," — "Rock of Ages cleft for me, *let me hide myself in Thee*," etc., etc., — taking turns in the privilege of song lest their united voices might be heard on the streets below — and with one of their number holding a guitar, that in case they were discovered, he might at once strike a national song while the rest joined in a dance of the province, a custom everywhere prevalent in Spain. Of these meetings Mr. Hall wrote:

"Thus they meet time after time, not knowing when they go in but they may be dragged out to prison and to death. Indeed, the week we left Malaga, one of them informed me that they had reason to believe they were suspected—and hence, as it would be perilous to gather again in town for their meetings, they should steal away to the mountains beyond the city till all excitement was over. * * * Among all this number of christians there are very few Bibles, but they read *together*, and wait patiently for *more light*."

That winter Matamoras went from his prison-cell in Barcelona to a dungeon in Grenada, and passing through Malaga took diligence in front of the principal hotel. A crowd of the popu-

lace gathered to see him go — but among them
all, though many were secretly his friends, not
a man or a woman dared even to *look* kindly
upon the shackled martyr, fearing the vigilant
scrutiny of the priests. These came from the
Cathedral and the University in a formidable
body, and glared upon their victim with wrath-
ful faces as he crept, with chained hands and
feet, attended by an officer, to the most obscure
seat among the luggage behind the driver's box.
The English and American travellers who looked
on from the balconies of the hotel saw a slight
figure pass through the densely packed masses,
and mount the diligence wheel.   The face shone
with more than human tenderness and courage,
and the hand — reaching its utmost — grasped
with a brother's sympathy, the manacled hand
of the culprit, whose only crime was ownership
of a New Testament, and faith in its message ;
and while another American and an English
friend repeated this act of fellowship, the brave
voice was distinctly heard above the muttered
anathemas of the crowd below, saying, "The
Lord be with you."

Then turning to Sir Robert Peel, who with
his family had seats that night for Grenada and

the Alhambra, he urged him to exert influence
with the Spanish government for the release of
Matamoras. Both Sir Robert and Lady Peel
visited the poor prisoner in his dungeon, and
earnestly endeavored to loosen his chains, — also
reporting his case to the British Crown — so that
Queen Isabella was finally compelled by the voice
of nations to relieve his sentence to banishment.
But the Great Ruler of all had prepared for
him a nobler release. The dungeon damps had
sapped his life, and though he went to Switzerland, he soon slept the long peaceful slumber in
the lovely God's-acre on the heights of Lausanne,
while the truth he scattered still lives on the
low-lands of his beloved Spain.

That winter was crowded with events of thrilling interest. One night, hearing an unusual
noise in the corridor of the hotel outside his
rooms, he listened for a moment, when a whis-
per arrested more closely his attention. Spaniards
who well knew the way, had sent two of their
number with a message which they softly breathed
through the key-hole into his ever-open ear:
"Señor A. has escaped from prison at Grenada"
(another criminal charged with heresy,) — "and
is hidden with the brethren here. We ask you

to spend the night in prayer with us, that he may escape before the officers overtake him." There were no foreign steamers due, but prayer was faithfully offered. Early next morning, an English steamer, in passing, *unexpectedly dropped anchor in the harbor.* From the break-water near the lighthouse a skiff pushed off — a muffled figure at the stern quietly boarded her, — and when, *twenty minutes later*, an armed and mounted guard came flying through the city, the British flag waved over the pursued man, while he safely steamed out to sea."

In April, having tarried through March at Gibraltar and Tangier on the African coast, Mr. Hall again entered Spain through Cadiz, and proceeded to Seville. On the day of his arrival there a Spanish acquaintance from Malaga surprised him on the street, who quickly glanced around to see if he was observed, then hastily delivered his message — and was lost in the crowd. This friend had anxiously awaited his coming — had left Malaga with his family, apparently like multitudes who were pouring into the city to witness the imposing *Santa Semana* ceremonies — but had really come to ask intercession of this American friend for the release of more than twenty brethren then lying in prison in Seville, on suspicion of heresy. He had but a moment — it might be death to be seen speaking to the "American heretic," as the priests called this protestant stranger, — but seizing his hand, with tears rolling over his swarthy face, he exclaimed, looking upward : " *Gracias, muchas gracias, Señor* — *In otro mundo! in otro mundo! mio amigo, y hermano en el Señor Jesu Christo* — *in otro mundo! in otro mundo!*" and darted out of sight.

Mr. Hall soon gave the facts to the acting American consul, a Scotch protestant gentleman, who doubted their accuracy, — but going together to the prison they found the prisoners, and succeeded by slow but persistent measures in securing some privileges and comforts for the unfortunate families — though not release. They were liberated in 1869, when Queen Isabella abdicated — and when the new government proclaimed liberty of conscience and of worship — and let fly on their hinges all prison doors.

From Malaga Mr. Hall wrote to friends in America, referring to Matamoras. Protestant hearts gave thanks for the faith that lit his face with smiles, as he acknowledged their greeting —and that strengthened him to wave a hopeful gesture of his manacled hand, as he turned away to a dungeon. * * * Thus

José Matamoras went to his judgment hall in this nineteenth century of the christian era. We wait with deep interest the result, but we fear he is foredoomed.

Many christians in Grenada, as well as in Barcelona and Malaga, in all several hundred, are waiting with intense anxiety the result of that trial. If he escapes with his life, in exile, they must still keep their faith a secret. If, as they strongly hope, he has the freedom of his own country, they will at once declare themselves. * * *

MALAGA, JANUARY 1, 1861.—After the recent heavy Atlantic storms we were glad to hear that our last letters did not go to the sharks. The month of age *our* mails get before they reach us is hard enough to bear, without the loss of those we send in return, but better than Mr. G's experience in Micronesia, who said of their yearly mail, when at date of writing he was reading a file of the Independent of the previous year, just come to hand, "You can little understand the shock with which the combined fifty-two jets of light and knowledge come home to us." The climate is almost perfect. Our doors and windows are wide open during day and night, inside our outer barrier. There is no dew, and hence no dampness. We have not needed fires since we came, in November, while at Nice the thermometer has stood at 6° above, and thoughout France and England at freezing point for days in succession. Indeed, sixteen leagues interior, and even in Grenada, we hear of ice forming without melting for three days. We see snow on the mountains thirty miles west—but this entire vega is green with vegetables, fruits, and flowers in all stages of growth. To-day bands are playing on the Alameda, and the air is balmy as June. This morning we sent Antonio for a carriage, that we might visit a private garden on the vega outlying the city, for which pleasure we had long held pressing invitation from the wealthy proprietor. We were amused when Antonio returned "by special permission with the one livery coach reserved for town drives"—and descended from our apartments in expectation of a grand turn-out. You should have seen us as we took our seats at the door of the Fonda. But the drive compensated all lack of equipage, and we went through fields of grain just springing up—beside acres of peas in blossom—with fig and almond trees starting new leaf, buds and flowers—along miles of geranium and cactus hedge—and under a sky as clear as Italy ever saw. To-morrow we propose to try the "country carriage" for a drive to Torre Molina, a village six miles on the coast—not only that we may see the country, but also the vehicle, after our droll experience with the "town" establishment.

This reminds me of our experience in Grenada. We were resting a few days under the very shadow of the Alhambra, and being almost oppressed with its varied wonders, we proposed one morning a drive to the Cartuja convent, so celebrated for its rich collection of marbles,—and so sent Bensaken for a carriage. No vehicle, good, bad or indifferent, can be obtained for less than $4.00 the trip. Ask one for an hour, half hour, or entire day, the charge is the same ; the philosophy of which tariff I am informed is this : "I must keep my carriage in repair all the season, and my horses well fed. Many days pass in which I cannot let them at all. Whoever takes them pays me not only for his own time, but also for my trouble."

GRENADA, JANUARY, 1861. * * * While strolling beneath the walls of that enchanted palace, the magnificence of which Irving has so gracefully described, I frequently came upon an old Moor, a noble representative of that race whose power was once as brilliant as supreme in all that portion of the Iberian Peninsula. The air of the man attracted me. His very step indicated a purer than Castilian blood ! His bowed form, and his sad, proud countenance, as he sat down to rest at the fountain of the great Gate of Justice, reminded me of those, who centuries before sat weeping beneath the willows of their early homes.

Aben Hassan, although past his three-score, welcomed with undisguised pleasure a representative from the home of Irving, —the historian of Moorish greatness. What he said of an ancestry richer than Medici or Bourbon ; of his rightful kingdom, more lovely than any equal area on the continent ; or of his hate of Spanish power which had overthrown and trampled upon the dearest privileges of his race, it is not my purpose here to write.

"I never get tired of this place," said he, as he came tottering up from the city through the long avenue of English elms,

" my heart beats stronger, sir, as I tread here the hallowed ground of my family." Our conversation turned to the causes that led to the bitter result, and thence, naturally, to Catholicism as it now exists in Spain. " Yes," said he in answer to my question, " I am a Roman Catholic in name. We Moors, though outcasts in Spain, are forced to subordination to the church, if we would remain by the graves of our fathers ; but I never go to confessional; I eat when and what I choose ; I do as others do. It is true every person must be subject to the church ; but a little money placed in the hands of a certain dignitary here purchases complete absolution. I am comparatively safe." Then glancing quickly around to see whether any one could hear him, in a subdued voice he whispered, " Sir, I am *not* a Catholic." He continued, " More than thirty years ago I was standing at the door of a hotel in the city below us, on the arrival of the Seville diligence, and saw a pale, sickly-looking Englishman alight ; to this hour I remember how his uneasy, blue eyes seemed to read my heart in its glance. Two weeks had passed, during which we had become somewhat familiar, when George Borrow took me to his room and told me *why* he came to Spain—and that he wished me to help him in the distribution of Bibles, a number of which he had with him. I *did* help him. He has gone to his *rest*. There are but ten Bibles remaining in the city. These are kept concealed except when read by stealth, being loaned from one to another among those who love the truth as it is in Jesus." * * *

The old Moor's story was the truth, as I afterward learned from other sources. Aben Hassan is one of more than two hundred humble believers in Jesus, who in that palatial city are regularly organized in their belief. Many of these I have met who are persecuted almost to death. Christians are hunted from city to city—even parents informing the Priests against their own children.

Who will not pray that both Moor and Spaniard may soon work together openly—rejoicing in the faith once delivered to the saints.

MALAGA, JANUARY 29, 1861.—(Referring to financial disaster at home.)—All has been ordered or permitted by One who knows what is best—and there I can leave it. All I ask is health for my family and myself, and God with me, I fear not the future. I write this from under bamboo shade, on a hillside overlooking the sea—where we frequently resort with our books, within the enclosure just above the terrace of burial places in the lovely English cemetery. I cannot give you a just idea of the beauty of this portion of Andalusia. Just around us are fig, olive, pepper and almond trees filled with singing birds—hedges of cactus and aloe which here grow to eight or ten feet—multitudes of flowers which we call exotic— and towering far above, right and left, are the snowy caps of the Ronda and Nevada mountains—while the blue Mediteranean without a ripple, spreads herself at our feet. * * * Yesterday we drove four miles out to the Roman aqueduct, built before the christian era, and intended to conduct the waters of the Ronda mountains across the Guadalhorce River for the supply of Malaga. It is more than a mile in length, and supported by massive masonry, but of course a ruin.

A fine harbor enables us to take an early sail or row before our breakfast ; and during the day, in this exceptionally dry climate, we enjoy open air rambling, reading, or writing, any where along the southern slopes of the hills fronting the sea.

* * * There was a funeral service on Thursday for a wealthy resident of the city. One hundred boys in mourning gowns, and bearing lighted candles as long and almost as large as themselves, led the procession ; and leading *them* were four boys carrying huge lanterns draped with black, and mounted with silver crosses ; one boy leading them all and holding a large wooden cross high up before him. After these came seventy priests in mourning badges,—and following them twelve *majos* to whom mourning suits had been given by the family bereaved. These also carried lighted candles. Then the bare casket on an elevated standard. Behind this a multitude of citizens on foot. Following these, twenty-eight empty private carriages, with wheels muffled in crape, completed the funeral cortège, which wound out of the city to the Campo Santa in the suburbs.

JANUARY 23.—This is the day of the Patron Saint of Toledo, when in the Cathedral of that city she will descend with her host of angels upon the altar. As no particular notice is given of the occasion here, other than the reading of an extra prayer, it will not be our privilege to witness any part of the pageant. * * * Just at this moment, from the balcony where I am writing, I see a woman passing up the Alameda with a basket of articles for sale on one arm, a stout boy on the other, and a roll of straw-matting on her head. We often see men and women carrying loads that an American horse would groan under—and the best of day laborers consider themselves well paid at ten cents a day, *and find themselves.* The *find* is a sop of bread in a stew of olive oil and garlic—with figs and native wine—and a siesta whenever they are inclined—besides cigarettes continually. But oh ! the beggars, who never labor at all. Murillo especially delighted in beggars, dwarfs, cripples, and other abnormal specimens of humanity—and he had no need to visit hospitals for his studies. They crowd every street corner. and interrupt the visitor at every doorway. From our hotel windows we can any morning count from twelve to thirty stationed around the front entrance to catch a pittance of passers-by. One morning I counted *thirty-two women* sitting on the curbing directly under our balcony, all of them in rags, and all of them professional beggars.

In a conversation with Bensaken, at Grenada, last month, upon these wretched creatures, he explained the honor of mendicant life, by giving the ground of caste distinctions. "Blue blood " is pure Castilian, and is only sustained by intermarriage with itself. "Red blood" is respectable, but never noble. Even royalty intermarrying with the possessors however remote, of income *not inherited*, loses caste to the latest generation. "White blood" is the stigma upon slightest admixture of Moorish pedigree.

To illustrate the force of this system of caste upon the people, let me give you the case of Espartero, that bold and successful leader in the cause of the present Queen, to whom, after his grand successes she offered, in gratitude, whatever he might desire at her hands. "Grant me a title," instantly replied her commander-in-chief. "That is beyond my power," sadly replied the Queen, "*your mother sold doves.*"

This state of affairs explains to us the premium on beggary and idleness—accepted by multitudes from the nobility, whose princely estates were generations ago wasted by wars or excesses. In some cities these go about on horseback, loftily begging their daily bread ; and if the " blue bloods " are content to live on charity, why should not the wretched dregs of humanity that swarm everywhere throughout the land, feel proud to put themselves in the ranks of such a leadership. One can easily count from one to five hundred of them in a single day's observation—and the majestic air with which they receive the *dinero* occasionally offered, is amusing.

MALAGA, FEBRUARY 13. * * * To-day we have been four hours by boat to the little town of Paulo and back, in season for dinner at 4 o'clock, served in our own parlor—where we also take our breakfasts at 9 A. M., after our morning row in the harbor. Just now the *Terral* or northwest wind is blowing, which seriously affects the nervous system. It is so irritating to Spaniards that criminal trials are decided with reference to prevalence of this wind.

* * * The priests are, many of them, undeniably and horribly corrupt, and those who have respect for their office do not extend it to their persons. A Spanish gentleman of education and high position in Andalusia, and a sincerely devout romanist, told me he would not allow the visits of their resident priests at his home, except in case of sickness or death, lest the reputation of his wife and daughters might suffer.

Queen Isabella is a scandal to her sex. Her influence is felt for evil throughout the court and the country. Happily, her civil power was in a measure limited by the "constitution" adopted, I believe, in 1848—and by the circulation of the Bible during a brief period just previous to that year. Now, no other than the catholic worship is tolerated. Circulation of scriptures, or preaching by protestants has a death penalty. The English Consul in Malaga, after long continued exertions, has just obtained permission to hold English service in his own house, which *foreigners* may attend. Within a few years, and through great difficulties, he obtained a grant from the government for a protestant cemetery here—the only protestant burial place in Spain. Hitherto, all heretics were taken down to the sea, and hastily buried at low tide. This cemetery is a lovely spot, admirably planned, and is shaded by the graceful

pimento and other ornamental trees.   Several Americans lie
buried here.

KINGDOM OF MOROCCO, TANGIER, AFRICA, MARCH 11, 1861.
(Year of Mahomet, 1288 ; month Charon ; twenty-eighth day.)
* * * Our stay in Spain, mostly thus far in Malaga, gave us
opportunity to test with tolerable fairness, what has been called
the most perfect climate on the face of the earth.   With snow-
covered mountains in sight, and with all northern Europe suffering an extraordinary degree of cold and snow, we enjoyed
the mildness, the fruits, and the flowers of the tropics—never
at any time needing fires nor winter clothing—though for the
social aspect of a cheering blaze we occasionally burned fragments of grape vine, and stumps of cactus hedge, large enough
when kindled in the morning to burn slowly all day and evening.   These we enjoyed in an open Franklin stove, *from Albany*,
N. Y., in our little parlor at Malaga, no other fuel but charcoal
being at command.   The uniform temperature is explained by
reference to the range of high mountains which effectually shut
off cold northerly winds from this paradise of vegetation,—as
also to the frontage on the Mediterranean on the south, receiving thence the hot winds of the African desert, tempered to
the balminess of Spring in the passage across the sea.

Last week, to escape the excessive heat of March in Malaga,
we left for Gibraltar, and from thence came across the Straits
to Tangier, to enjoy, briefly, the marvelous climate of this
northern promontory of Africa.   Our luminous track that
night, through the phosphorescent currents of the sea was
wonderful ; and the brilliant light of Jupiter crowning the
grim outline of the rock as we lay at anchor in the morning
twilight under the shadow of Gibraltar, was a fitting climax to
our delight.

With all the advantages of the climate of Andalusia combined, we gain here, besides the tempering influence of Atlantic breezes upon the sultry heats of Spring, which on the Spanish side, east of Gibraltar, become almost intolerable at this
season—the healing influence of resinous shrubs growing abun-
dantly on the table lands outlying the town.   The aroma from
these permeates the atmosphere, and has wonderful power,
especially in pulmonary affections.   We are told of several

almost miraculous cures effected by this climate, and we already perceive a soothing element in the spicy breath of the interior winds, beyond anything we have realized in the pineries or tar-producing regions of our own country. The air is also perfumed with the delicious fragrance of orange and lemon groves belonging to the different consulates, of which there are fourteen in all,—and the paths to the gardens are hedged in by immense aloes and prickly pears, overrun by rose vines and other trailing flowers.

With Tangier and its surroundings we are delighted. By five hours steaming to be transferred from a civilized to a barbarous people—to be set down, as in a dream, among glittering mosques, and majestic Moors, and in daily view of the camel-trains and wild Arabs of the desert, as they go in and out of the city gates with merchandise for Fez, or for Gibraltar, gives all the stimulus so strange a people with their habits and customs should supply to invalids who need diversion. Our consul-general, Mr. Brown, has shown us marked attention—has given us every facility for seeing the city and the people with safety, and under favoring circumstances.

Our hotel is near the American Consulate on *Washington street*. The stalwart Moors, who seized our luggage at landing, hurried on, and stood with it around the entrance arch-way of this hotel, waiting for "backsheesh,"—while we were finding our way through the almost hopeless windings of the narrow streets.

We have tried the speed of the famous Arab *barbs*, and the novelty of a camel-ride ; have visited the wild-boar haunts so celebrated among English sportsmen,—and for shorter trips have visited Carthagenian and Roman ruins within sight of the walls,—and have also witnessed the frightful contortions of a snake charmer with his basket of venemous reptiles. We find ourselves in the midst of a peaceable people, content with trade between themselves and the Jews, who have settled here in large companies, since they were expelled from Spain. Their only imports are from Gibraltar, which they consider their rock of defense against the armies of the opposite continent. The sad persecutions of the Spaniards have wearied them of war of conquest—and of course with a rich country in possession they shrink from war of defense. How long they can remain unmolested is a question of interest—for Spain seems to be doing her utmost to provoke them by unrighteous extortions, to an open contest. She already holds Tetuan, and has a temporary claim upon Algiers.

Slavery exists in the kingdom of Morocco, though in a milder form than in America. The Moors are devout worshippers of Mahomet, and of course Friday is their Sabbath. The Jews gather to their synagogues on Saturday,—and on Sunday, there being no organized christian worship in the city—not even at the consulates—we go outside the walls, to a bluff overlooking the sea, and sing our praises "on Afric's golden sands."

SEVILLE, APRIL, 1861. * * * From Tangier to Gibraltar, some forty miles across the Straits, and thence, after visiting the fortifications and the excavated galleries of the rock, by steamer to Cadiz, the cleanest city of its size I have visited. Its location on a peninsula, bounded on the south by the Atlantic, and on the north by the river Guadalete, gives a fine harbor and an excellent sewerage. Murillo left some of his choicest works here, but during the peninsular war many of them were removed. He lies buried beneath the painting upon which he was at work when the falling of a scaffolding caused his death.

* * * The religious confraternities throughout Spain hold immense wealth in robes and jewels, and life-size figures of the Blessed Virgin, the Saviour, the Apostles, and the Saints. These they display in processions, during the ceremonies of Holy Week. The brotherhood in Seville are exceptionally rich in these possessions, and their processions this year included their entire list, and was the most imposing that has been witnessed in Spain for many years. One little wooden image of the Virgin owns diamonds alone to the value of millions of dollars—the front view of which, as this goddess was paraded through the streets on the shoulders of men who walked beneath the draperied platform on which she sat enthroned, was one blaze of light from her forehead to her feet

The servile reverence of the masses for the "sacred images" displayed in these processions is pitiable indeed,—for all ages and all classes of the people fall on their knees and remain prostrate while the slow pomp and magnificence are passing. But underneath this surface there is another state of feeling arising—day-break is coming for poor Spain !

A few years ago, Espartero and a few other bold spirits determined on a change of government, which included many reforms, and Isabella was put forward as their representative. To this movement was opposed Don Carlos, heir to the throne by regular descent, and by nearly the entire priesthood. The adventurers succeeded—a constitution was adopted—a congress was elected—convents were destroyed—and the influence of monasteries was materially lessened—priestly power and income were reduced—old Spain seemed about to lift the veil ! But true to her lineage, Isabella soon dismissed her liberal advisors ; and she is to-day surrounded by the faithful, more than ever vigilant for the Papal rule. Preaching and reading the scriptures have now a death penalty—yet the gospel *is* preached—and the scriptures *are* circulated—and in Malaga alone there are over one hundred and fifty reformers, who are ready at the first note of liberty to declare themselves. For these, sacerdotal agents are continually on the watch. Only a few days before I left Malaga, a house adjoining our hotel being suspected of heresy, was searched by the papal police.

I have reason to know that in the cellar of an obscure house in Malaga, a printer, whose legitimate use of his press gave the city a daily paper, is now nightly toiling to print such fragments of scripture as he can stealthily strike off between sun and sun—from a Testament he received at the hands of a foreigner ; and his little son of *eight years* not only helps to circulate them by day among their company of believers, but begs to share the labors of the night ; and under cover of the darkness, night after night when he ought to be sleeping, this noble child sets type with unwearied hands and brave heart, to help the great work on. Such is the spirit of which martyrs are made !

CORDOVA, APRIL, 1861. * * * It is amazing that a civilized people can submit for generations to be so entirely humbugged by their priests. In the churches are gathered the bones of *thousands* of Saints,—each separate bone religiously preserved in a glass case, and perhaps surrounded with pearls

5

and precious stones. In some of the larger cases are entire skulls, the hollow eye-sockets filled with faded artificial flowers and other tawdry trappings. One of the richest chapels in Seville holds over two thousand of these "sacred relics." Around the shrines where these are deposited are hung models in wax, of arms, legs, eyes, feet, hands, or any other part of the human frame whose diseases have been cured by intervention of these miraculous bones.

In the convent La Victoria, at Malaga, is kept on the high altar, a miraculous image of the Virgin which heads the yearly processions of the priests when they pray for rain, and also when they intercede for the withholding of supply. As rain seldom falls in this southern section of Spain during the seven months preceeding November, the priests are shrewd enough to arrange their exhibitions of this image when the elements are prepared to yield moisture, and the poor deluded people think "our lady" really controls the clouds in answer to prayer.

On a high hill in the rear of Convent La Victoria is a beautiful little chapel, the rugged path leading to it adorned with numerous white crosses which mark the *Via Crucis* or way of the cross. Over this the women of Malaga go on their knees in penance, saying the prayers prescribed at the confessional, in the cathedral, or the parish church. This *Via Crucis* is seen on the outskirts of every considerable city of Spain, and multitudes of women trail themselves and their sins through the dust for miles for this sort of absolution.

MADRID, APRIL, 1861.—Every town has its guardian saint— 'and every family has its special Saint-day, on which it is etiquette to pay visits of ceremony. Indeed, every day is a Saint-day, duly announced in the papers,—but a general feast day comes not oftener than once in two weeks, excepting the Sabbaths, all of which after morning mass, are given up to music, promenading, bull-fights, or gathering at the theatres and casinos. On a given day in December, St. Anthony blesses all donkeys and horses, *and if the prayers offered to him by the priests are sufficiently well paid* he also restores lost articles, especially lost traveling luggage. He might do well to establish a branch office in the United States.

Of the miraculous image of the Virgin in the Atocha convent, in this city, so much has been said and written that I need not describe either her magnificent wardrobe or her healing powers. In the Seville cathedral, under the high altar, are kept the veritable garments of the Virgin of Nazareth, with bits of the bones and of the cross of our Saviour. A robed priest will exhibit these for a peseta—and will also display a crucifix made from a nugget of gold brought by Columbus on his return from the New World.

Spain is rich in architecture and in ruins—and has also great treasure in paintings. In Madrid is the choicest gallery of paintings in Europe, north of Rome. Murillo's best works are in Seville—and of these, besides the collection in the Museo, those he most prized still hang on the walls of his own house—and among them an Ecce Homo surpassing even Guido's in poise and expression ; and of his pictures in Madrid, his master-piece, St. Elizabeth healing diseases, is not in the grand collection, but in the Academia, in Calle de Alcala.

BURGOS, APRIL 22.—A Christian and a Jew while at work together in a vineyard were disputing regarding their religions —when the Jew said to the Christian, "I will believe your religion when I see a Christ come out of a vine-stalk"—and behold ! a Christ at once appeared. The wonder was noised abroad. This image, about five inches long, was taken with pomp to the cathedral in Valladolid, and was placed in a temple of silver weighing 22,000 ounces ; and there we saw it under a canopy of gold, where it is worshipped by thousands for its miraculous power. Even the University of Valladolid, with its more than thousand students, is not so celebrated as this fruit of the vine.

BURGOS.—In this city, in a sacred chapel of the cathedral, there is a stained and dingy wooden image of the Saviour carved by Nicodemus when the living model was before him, which was originally set up in Jerusalem, but it preferred the more devoutly religious atmosphere of Spain, and found its own way to the sea, and navigated itself through the counter currents of the Mediterranean and Atlantic till it appeared in the Bay of Biscay, where a merchant of Burgos found it, and placed it in the convent of St. Augustine. There it at once commenced to work miracles. At one time it raised ten men from the dead. The prelates of the cathedral coveted so rich a treasure, and twice they captured it, but it immediately returned itself, unaided, to its old quarters. Since the suppression of convents, however, it has been content to occupy the cathedral chapel, where it has been visited with imposing ceremonies by all the Kings and Queens of Spain—and by the royal family of Naples, who have given it immense sums of treasure. It stretched out its hands to Isabella the catholic, on occasion of her visit, after the conquest of Grenada,—and on the anniversary of the crucifixion it *always* sweats great drops of blood. *All this is true,* for volumes have been written in testimony of its wonderful life. Men and women from all parts of Spain make pilgrimage to this shrine, bringing children to be blessed, and diseases to be cured—and the votive offerings of clothing, and wax models, hanging over the walls of the chapel where this miraculous image now stands, reminds one of a ragfair. Pilgrims who were kneeling before it, at date of our visit, told me they had traveled on foot four hundred miles to receive its blessing.

A —— asked the attending priest if the pretty little wax models were ever sold to visitors, as souvenirs. "Oh, no Señora," with a grieved and horrified expression, "they are *forever holy*—and even when by reason of age they fall in fragments, the particles are all reverently gathered, and melted into candles for the most sacred services of the cathedral." To test the veracity of our scandalized friend, I slipped a generous bit of silver into his hand, at the same moment pointing to a really pretty wax model of a baby's head, suspended by a ribbon near the railing—when seizing the money with alacrity, he gave the significant Spanish shrug, and then with equal alacrity laid the "forever holy" relic before me.

BURGOS.—The cathedral here is richer in bas-reliefs and statues—in pure gothic arches and effects of light and shadow than any other church we have seen in Spain, except the cathedral at Seville. I entered the building first at twilight. Far away at an altar a score of priests were chanting before a brilliantly lighted figure of the Virgin, and they were surrounded by hundreds of kneeling worshippers. The music was softened by distance, but yet *full* from many echoes. As I lingered, I was able to discern the forms of many others kneeling near the walls and columns, and occasionally a sombre figure flitted past me to the chapel of some patron saint.

Next morning we went again to the cathedral, and were soon lost in study of the bas-reliefs in marble—a series of masterly art. Suddenly a hand was laid on my shoulder, and a priest in his robes said hurriedly at my side, "Kneel to the Host! Kneel to the Host!" A glance toward the high altar showed me that High mass was being celebrated—and that I had unconsciously lingered too near, so absorbed had I been in admiration of the sculpture before me. Sincerely begging pardon for disturbing the worship, I prepared at once to withdraw. "No, no," said the priest, "you cannot go away—you must kneel to the Host." "But I *cannot* kneel to the host, for I do not believe it is really the body of Christ. I am very sorry I disturb you—I will go away till the service is over." "No, no, you must *kneel.*" "But I *cannot* kneel, I should act a lie." "But you *shall* kneel." "I will *not* kneel." "The Holy Church *compels* you to kneel." "No church can compel me to kneel, I will *die* first."

By this time the passion of the priest knew no bounds, and with oaths and imprecations he followed me to the door, toward which I steadily and calmly took my way, sorry indeed that I had not noticed the elevation of the Host in season to retire, which is my custom in catholic churches—but not in the least intimidated by the threats of my persecutor. Finally, as I passed the threshhold, he had the satisfaction of shaking his fist in the face of the American heretic, whom he dared not lay hands upon, I scarcely know why. I asked in my heart, that he might soon receive *large measure* of the spirit of the Blessed Master whose *sacred presence* he was so profanely guarding.

This Basque country is the old Kingdom of Navarre, mountainous but fruitful. The people are a hardy, industrious race—with language and customs distinct from the Spaniards. They have no written literature. It is said that in their dialect the written word Solomon might be pronounced Nebuchadnezzar.

The only line of railway yet opened in Spain is built by English capitalists, from Cadiz, through Seville, to Cordova—

with a gap of diligence ride thence to Manzanares,—and then rail to Madrid. There is a branch road from Madrid to Alicante on the coast, over which trains are run whenever passengers or freight are sufficient. We take diligence to-morrow from Burgos, three days over the Pyrenees to Bayonne in France.

PARIS, MAY 6. * * * The news that comes almost daily of our national affairs, is startling. We who left the States at peace can hardly comprehend the rapid progress of events to the actual unsheathing of arms. There is but one feeling here in regard to these difficulties. "Our sympathies and our hopes are with the right, and with the United States," asserts the Siecle—the leading government organ of France.

Said a distinguished Frenchman to me a few days since, "That first gun fired at Fort Sumpter was the knell of African slavery in your country—mark my word."

Individuals of every class express their wonder that civilized men should be so mad with passion as to place themselves at such fearful odds, with the moral, intellectual, financial and constitutional power of the United States, and of the world, against them. "What madness,"—"what folly," and like expressions attend the announcement in the French papers of the belligerent advances of the South. Even the Spaniards think the South must be insane. I confess to no little solicitude for the future. I pray that no more blood be shed. Still I trust that this question of African slavery shall now and forever know its limits.

V.

Financial Integrity.

There is nothing in the universe that I fear but that I shall not know all my duty, or shall fail to do it.—*Mary Lyon.*

" The principle is of universal application that every thing that is dishonorable is in process of defeat, and everything that is manly is in process of success. Depend upon it, there is nothing like being able to look the world in the face and say, " my record is honest, and cannot be touched ; my hands are clean."

" There is the truest courage, I think, in adjusting ourselves to circumstances. If God bereaves us, let us live bereaved. If He takes a blessing from us, let us do without it,—not with stoicism, but with child-like submission. ' Father, you know best.' "

The years 1856 to 1859 were years of peril to mercantile interests, — and the importing house in which Mr. Hall was the junior partner felt the shock and the danger. Men of judgment said disaster was averted only through the almost superhuman exertions he made to keep the business from sinking.* When the firm was again on a safe basis he felt the reaction, and preferring to retire from a position of so varied cares, he proposed to withdraw his name, but to leave his capital for another year, thus giving time to supply the vacancy without detriment to the associated interests. The reply was prompt and earnest. "Take your capital if you prefer, but leave your name. That is worth more to us than money."

When, a few months later, Mr. Hall was called to Europe, he carefully adjusted his finances — knew from personal examination the exact assets and liabilities of the business house — held in his pocket memoranda of the same — and though entirely satisfied of clear sailing, so zealously guarded the rights of his partners that he arranged for traveling and family expenses outside his business income, that they might not for a moment have reason to feel themselves trammeled or depleted by one not actively with them.

On the deck of the steamer, just before she sailed, one of these gentlemen took his hand with emphatic assurance of "plain sailing for the ship at home," and urged him with apparent candor and cordiality to drop all concern for their common welfare, to take "a much needed rest." This was in October.

Before January of that winter he received let-

ters in Malaga announcing suspension of the
house. His brief and emphatic comment was,
"it is a dishonest failure." This opinion he
never had cause to modify. What he suffered
during the months that followed — not that in
an evil hour a competency had been swept away,
but that his fair name was compromised in dark
transactions while he was too far off either to
investigate or to establish defense — is known
only to Him before whom he poured out all the
anguish of his injured soul.

In the following Spring, as soon as it was
safe for the invalid for whose life he had left
New York, he hastened to Paris, en route to
America, saying, " I shall now probe this matter
to the bottom." But the evening before he was
to leave for London and Liverpool, dispatches
from family friends called him to the bedside of
an uncle in Genoa. He obeyed the summons,
and repressing all his own harrowing griefs, he
helped by day and night watchings to soothe the
last hours of this dear relative, who lingered
till late Autumn, and then slept in the quiet
cemetery above the Bay, overlooking the Mediterranean. This delay, inevitable as it was, only
deepened the shadows of aspersion set afloat in

New York; and when he finally returned he found some had been ready to hear insinuations that "he left the country to avoid what he knew was coming," — that "he drew so heavily on the house for his absence that they could not stand the pressure," — and that "he staid away after the failure because he was a coward and *dared* not come home."

On arrival in the city, in September, 1861, some of his best friends, including his family physician who had well guaged his sensitive organization, and a brother in the Tabernacle who was one of the heaviest creditors of the firm, called to advise him not to remain in New York — not to try in his condition of health to clear up so hopeless a ruin, but to strike out into a new field where with renewed strength of body he might retrieve his fortune. He replied, "Gentlemen, I thank you for your sympathy and proffered support, but I cannot take your advice. It is not my way. I shall stay in New York and face my creditors. I shall begin to-morrow, *and if there is a bottom to this affair I shall find it.*"

He never found it, though he used sharp instruments and cut deep and long; but he came

out of the search with clean hands. Then —
with impaired health, and wounded ambitions —
he began at zero, and pressed his way up
through his share of the liabilities of the house,
till one by one *he paid them all.* When he
declared his decision to undertake this struggle,
men who honored his integrity denounced an effort they considered fatal to his physical ener-
gies — urging his exemption from legal claims.
"The *Divine Law* is my guide," was his only
reply, and though he would never again accept
a business partner, his every enterprise was pros-
pered till the end was accomplished. His own
words ought here to bear testimony to the
bruising and the healing of this ordeal while at
the same time they show how cordially, in the
midst of all these troubles, he identified himself
with passing interests, doing ever "as unto the
Lord and not unto men" whatever offered to be
done.

Perhaps it should be mentioned that during
the winter of 1861–2, he was unanimously
elected deacon of the church he had so long
loved. This expression of the confidence of his
christian friends, while he was struggling under
the heavy pressure of financial reverses, was a

great surprise, and hence a four-fold solace to his sensitive spirit. How well he fulfilled that trust is known to many who walked with him in loving fellowship.

NEW YORK, NOVEMBER 29, 1861.—*No books yet.* I dare not say what I think till I go farther in the search. I am afraid there are dark transactions. In my own mind the chain is complete. Every day now more and more satisfies me that they who would have injured me have been powerless. Thanks to God that I have been restrained from taking any questionable step such as might have given us *means* at the sacrifice of *right.* I can lose money and bear it—but I cannot afford to be a dishonest man. I know not what is in reversion for me, but I do pray that I may never again be called to pass through the withering trials of the last few months. Pray for me that He who knows the end from the beginning will keep me in the right path.

NOVEMBER 30, 1861.—This a. m. went up to our Mission ground, vicinity of 54th street, in search of rooms to which the school may remove ; returning to service and communion at the Tabernacle. Fifty-eight united with our church by letter, and two by profession. The last communion was at Dr. Binney's chapel in London—with his wonderful sermon on the character and life of David. * * * After dinner went to Mission School—and then to my round of visits with the old ladies who are too infirm to get to church, and who expect me to drop in to read, and talk with them about the sermons, etc. You know the list.

DECEMBER 2, 1861. * * * Yesterday morning I went up to St. Luke's Hospital for a good talk with Dr. Muhlenburg about the right place for our new Mission. He is as earnest and zealous as always before, when I have met him, for the education of our children of the rocks.

DECEMBER, 1861. * * * Dr. Thompson gave us a searching sermon on the work of the Holy Spirit, and at 2, p. m., we went to Mission Sabbath School, at the new place, corner 6th avenue and 41st street.   The school came very near dying out, and the teachers were talking about giving it up.   I went from one to another with strong opposition to that—and then turning the other shoulder, I gave them all the encouragement I could.

DECEMBER, 1861.   *   *   *   To-day has been another of prolonged agony—and yet immensely relieved by the sympathy and confidence of creditors.   Never before have I felt the value of character ; still this is a heart-bruising.   *   *   *   I am anxious to make money enough *on this spot* to pay all we owe, and I shall do it before I die, God willing.   I am not crushed, but I confess to a considerable bleeding.   Only for my trust in God and —— I would rather die than to go through this ordeal.

FEBRUARY 13, 1862.   *   *   *   Burnside is now duly established, and the whole city is gay with flags.   *   *   *   I am making progress financially.   Pursuing the economies of the last few months, I shall be able to pay off a part of the firm indebtedness, and also my own rather heavy payments due within the next thirty days.   I know that like Thomas I am sometimes filled with doubts about my financial future.   I must pray more and study more than I have done.   Then all these things will be added.   I know I have relied too much on my own efforts.   I must look above for strength and guidance. Pray that I may become all I should be.

MARCH 1, 1862.   *   *   *   For two or three nights past I have been driving along the Mediterranean shores, and that magnificent scenery stands out bolder and grander than ever to my view.   Then to Madrid, and over the Guadarramas and the Pyrenees.   *   *   *   W. has reached the *what-for* age, and is full of questions, which must be patiently answered.   How easily we forget that we were once children, groping our way into light.

7th.   *   *   *   One year ago this evening we bade farewell to Malaga.   I think the topography of that city will never be obliterated.   In my thoughts I go wandering about its streets —along its shores—climbing its battlements day and night. To-night we are going to Gibraltar on the "Ville de Paris."

MARCH 8, 1862.   *   *   *   Have been able to meet several

payments this month. Sometimes when I look at the amounts still unpaid, and see the ease of my late partners in the enjoyment of what is not justly theirs, I feel rather discouraged. Still, I am getting on better than I anticipated, and better than most I know who have been unhorsed by reverses. If my health is spared I shall soon get clear of all my trammels.

MARCH 14, 1862. * * * J. writes that he has been appointed, by Gen. Burnside, as Medical Purveyor of Dep't of N. C. Headquarters, at present at Roanoke Island. The rebel Colonel, O. Jennings Wise, was under his care. He died without a murmur, on account of sufferings, and was a gentleman to the last, and apparently grateful for attentions ; but when asked, with intention, if possible, to find the exact location of the ball which had entered his lungs, in order to extract it—what was his position when the ball struck him, he promptly replied, "at the head of my men, Sir, facing the enemy."

APRIL 13, 1862. * * * Bible class and morning service. Prof. Park preached from the text, "When I awake I shall be satisfied." Just what my soul panted for ! After the close of sermon Dr. Thompson read the President's proclamation—and an appropriate psalm—the choir rendered a thrilling anthem, and then Dr. T. closed with a fervent prayer, and benediction.

JULY, 1862. * * * Senator —— weakened the administration and did himself great discredit in his speech last week. There is a class of men at the North, of which —— is one, and —— is another, who should be publicly whipped. One striving for fame and position,—the other, to gratify personal pique. Numbers more in pursuit of wild abstractions, are doing the Union serious injury. What is before us we know not, only that the Union *shall be preserved.* If slavery goes down with the war, let it be so. It will go down—for it must meet its doom sooner or later. That point is of minor relative importance now. The *Union* is what we have to do *with* and *for.* I look with disgust upon the miserable littleness that stops doggedly before any mole hill in the way of personal or party ambition, while Alps are to be scaled and overcome, *that a nation may be free.*

* * * I could bear the loss of property, but it did break down my spirits that there were those who tried to misrepre-

sent me—those who had received much at my hands. I had the blessing of a mind conscious of rectitude. Enemies had sown tares in my absence, but thanks to Him who cares for His children, the tares so diligently sown have not taken root. Each day I am more convinced that my character stands untarnished. Men assure me that hard as it was, it has given me greater hold on their confidence. * * * Thank Heaven! though I cannot to-day claim for my family a fortune, I can leave them an unsullied name. * * * A very special Providence has supported me. How do those men *live* who never pray? "Call upon me in the day of trouble, and I will deliver thee," is a precious command and promise. * * * I am thankful I do not stand in their places though I have lost all.

NANTUCKET, AUGUST 3, 1862. * * * Aunt S. was expecting me, and all gave me a cordial Cape Cod welcome. The aged aunt, for whom she lives, is in full possession of her faculties—is gentle and lovely—a saint, ready for the Master's call. The island is delightful. The salt air yesterday, as we had it by rail and by boat, was beyond expression welcome, and invigorating. The heat was intense when we left the city. Little ——— lay stretched on the sofa as I went into the library on that last terrible day—the hottest by the calendar, in forty years,—and exclaimed as I entered,—"why, I went out on the balcony a moment, and *I perspired seven times!*"

NEW YORK, APRIL, 1863. * * * The church should notice her young men *socially.* We must tone up not only the mercantile young men, but these young students whose influence in the professions is to be so vast on minds during the next thirty to fifty years. The grand work for us, I am satisfied, is among the young men of our congregations under thirty years of age. With few exceptions in our city churches, active work is relinquished at about thirty, leaving those below that age to be built up and strengthened in christian graces, or led to the Saviour, *by the few exceptions,* or by the unripe experience of very young christians, Let us all do what we can to influence this branch of christian effort. This mass of crude metal can become as burnished gold, *and we are set to watch the crucible.*

JULY, 1863. * * * When we shall be unclothed of mortality, and clothed upon of life enduring, how will our hearts be united in the nobler, holier labors for which we are in training here ! Sometimes I can almost see the portals opening. What joy in the thought of Heaven as our *home*—that when in the earthly life we have trained our children to walk aright, we may go on, and beckon them homeward ! Living thus, how can we feel that we have lived in vain !

AUGUST, 1863. * * * I go to sleep every night by fixing my thoughts on some place or route of our foreign wanderings. Last night I went down on the road from Genoa to Florence— to the beautiful white marble cross erected on the rock whence Garabaldi embarked "for the freedom and unity of Italy,"— now overhung with wreaths and festoons of fragrant flowers, placed there daily by the women of United Italy. Those from Venice frequently set in black, encircling some sigh for the liberty she has not yet realized,—thinking also of that purer cross built upon that sacred foundation, the "rock of ages"—once hung around with many sorrows,—now glorified ; to which all nations may come, for He who erected that cross has borne all our sorrows making us *all* free through His spirit.

AUGUST 9, 1863, SABBATH, P. M. * * * I cannot resist telling you I have been very near the Saviour this morning, and have felt the presence of the Spirit. I have endeavored to re-consecrate to Him all I have and all I am. Have been reading the closing chapters of Malachi, and have been thinking whether I have proved the fulfilment of the promises as I ought.

During all these years he pursued with unflagging interest and success, his loving ministries to the lonely, the afflicted, and the suffering. In the pressure of business claims, when an hour lost might be of vital moment — and harrassed as he was by his own uncertain finances, he was always ready to support by counsels, or by personal attentions, those on both continents, who looked to him in their day of trouble. Was it a mother, anxious over the uncertain fate of a wayward son — he set aside his own important affairs, and went day and night through a neighboring city in search of the prodigal, till in a remote suburb he was found. Was it a father, led astray by the wine when it is red in the cup — he followed him with unwearied zeal till he sat again clothed and in his right mind. Some of these can bear living testimony to his persistent vigilence while danger impended — as well as to his strong, sympathetic encouragement and friendly support after it was safely passed. His last drives in New York, in February of 1873, were stimulated by the hope of reclaiming an inebriate friend, and when entreated by his family not to waste his precious strength in so exhausting interviews, when the air of the Park would invigorate him, he replied, "I have not long to stay — and *perhaps he will be braver to overcome if he knows I am watching him.*"

He considered widows and orphans his especial charge, and through all his active life they received his generous care. Seeking them out to relieve their perplexities, whether rich or poor, he patiently listened and wisely advised. Had

6

they doubtful or troublesome investments — he assumed responsibilities on their behalf, or re-adjusted their finances or their securities without stint of effort, and without commission. Doubt-less in remembrance of this service in the Mas-ter's name, his own household will carry uncan-celled, through life, the sweet burden of gratitude for sympathy and counsel, so freely bestowed in memory of "the beloved disciple." Doubtless he knows and acknowledges the full measure of it all, in the great assembly of the redeemed, where he now walks in white.

In the Spring of 1865, Mr. Hall went south to avoid the return of a serious throat trouble — sailing March 11, on steamer "New York." Of this trip he wrote :

MARCH 12, 1865.—We have on board a very pleasant com-pany, including with civilians, Dr. C., U. S. Medical Inspector, —H. S. D., a prominent Boston lawyer,—a half dozen army surgeons,—two colonels of the regular army,—and one rebel general, a very interesting man,—with some three hundred soldiers, representing every State in the Union. As we could not have service on board, I spent a portion of the morning be-low talking with the soldiers, and have been much interested in them. Met, among others, several South Carolina deserters going home, having taken the oath.

PULASKI HOUSE, SAVANNAH, MARCH 14, 1865.—At Hilton Head I first set foot on the sacred soil—not a-la-Columbus. Af-ter going through the necessary forms, I took steamer up the Savannah river, five hours slow running to the city. There was with me a rebel Brigadier General on his return from Fort Delaware—having taken the oath,—a genial, agreeable man, who told me of each plantation as we passed. He was himself swept clean, in one day, of $300,000 worth of property—and gave me the names of planters, once owners of these islands, who are to-day in interior Georgia, penniless and homeless, who last year actually planted corn with their own hands to raise money to support their families. Sherman's army have driven them out.

I have not been here long enough to ascertain thoroughly the spirit of the people, but with unusual facilities I have conversed with many, and I have yet to find the first person who believes in the final success of the Confederacy.

MARCH 19, 1865.—This morning I attended Episcopal service in the church located by Oglethorpe himself. When Sherman was here (I have it from authority,) the Bishop's assistants waited on him to know if he should require them to pray for the President of the United States? "Pray for whom you please, gentlemen—pray for the Devil, if you choose, or for Jefferson Davis. I think one needs your prayers as much as the other." The gentlemen withdrew, and decided to omit in their prayers that entire part of the service.

Here is a great vanquished brotherhood. Can we not show them that we are not alone valiant in the support of principle on the battle-field, but that we are equally abounding in love and forgiveness. The sermon was a good one from the text, "the wages of sin is death." After dinner, putting my Bible in my pocket, I went down, designing to go out and read to some of the poor whites—but found waiting, Rev. Mr. M., who wished me to visit with him the colored Sabbath Schools, and I did so. Thence to a gathering of colored ministers and others who are planning evening study for adult males among the blacks. I saw and talked to-day with one woman who is learning to read, and can already spell words of one syllable. "I jes wants to learn to read de Bible—dats all I wants ; coz den, if I lub my Saviour, I shall see my chillen in Heben ; dat's what I hopes for." I could write pages of conversations, some amusing, some affecting,—all indicating the new life of this people.

* * * Through my friends and the military authorities, I learn that there are not less than 1400 white refugees, now here, drawing rations from the government. I have visited many families, and in all find the same story of destitution and gaunt poverty. For instance : This morning I passed an open window by which sat a woman with the *homeless* look in her face ; worn, half-vacant, utterly hopeless. She was ragged and barefooted. So was the child in her arms. She told me her story ; was once a teacher, born and reared in Georgia. Her husband a cripple, and helpless. Of her eight children, the oldest in the army, and unheard of for two years,—the other seven around her—dirty, uncombed, miserably clad ; one sick ; with difficulty had kept the breath of life in him during the night just past. She took me to him in a little, dark room adjoining, where the poor child of eight or ten years lay gasping in a mass of rags as wretched as himself.

In the same room with this woman sat another, a widow, with six children—all of them clean, but she was listless and sad. Her husband had been conscripted, and was dead. Both of these families, living together in *one small room*, were forced to leave the country and come to Savannah, for fear of rebel guerillas and bands of blacks, who are devastating the land. They had no furniture—not even beds or bedding—no wood— and very few cooking utensils. It was the barest existence I ever saw.

In one room of a large, old rebel hospital, on which the guard told me his men had already spent fifty days' hard labor in order to its proper cleansing, I found a widow with one child. Husband had been in the army and was dead. She was born in England—was fore-woman for B., in New York, for five years. Married a Georgian at Atlanta. Owned two houses there—one was destroyed by a shell—the other was burned to the ground. Has nothing left but her child—not even a bed. Is tidy, intelligent, uncomplaining.

Another room in same building—with two bricks and a basin for furniture—holds two rebel deserters from Lee's army. Came over from lower Georgia with a squad of men. Cannot read nor write—have heard nothing from their families in many months. Must stay here till they find some way to get home. Love Lee—hate Davis ; "would shoot Davis quicker than they would a fox or a Yankee."

In still another room, I found as furniture a rough board platform, and on it an old quilt. Wrapped up in the latter was a poor, wretched creature, from the lowest strata of humanity with one child "up country, somewhar." Says she only wants a bed to make her happy.

In room No. 5, six deserters on foot 160 miles, from Augusta, —and in the last which I visited a desolate woman without furniture, or dish, or even a blanket, and " without a friend on the face of the earth."

The guard who accompanied me says words cannot express the degradation and misery of these poor creatures, and the city is full of them. I shall endeavor in some way to relieve all *these* cases, and others that have come to my knowledge. Government, as you know, can give no more than rations ; but what *is* to be done with these hundreds, not to exceed one in five of whom can read or write ?

* * * I stood last night among a crowd of negroes who were viewing the first colored regiment of Charleston, just arrived here. A regiment, by the way, of first-class men—jet black, and under perfect discipline. As I stood on the Quincy granite steps of the Custom House and saw them pass to our national airs. and with prompter step than half our own New York militia would give, I thought of Toombs, who has not *yet* been proclaimed the Moses of the black race, nor called his slaves to the crack of his whip *on Bunker Hill.* I said to one of the negroes beside me, " The boys do look brave enough to fight. Are you going into the ranks ?" " Going ? *Yes, Sar,* I goes into de 'trenchments right away. No white man tell nigger now he can't learn *tat-tics.* Our old Father Abra*h*am has got de men, now ! *de nation am saved !* "

Walking up the street yesterday with a friend, a former slave holder, worth before the war nearly a million, and who, after Sherman passed through was not worth a dime—indeed, he told me his inventory at that date reported one chicken and one dove—and who was, I know, one of the kindest of masters— he called out to a black across the street, " John, is that you ?" The fellow saw him but did not reply. He cried again, " *John,* is that *you?*" The negro, half turning, replied, "*No sa-ar*, I'se not John," and passed on ; my friend adding to me with no stint of emphasis, "That rascal says he does not know me, *but he does.* He belonged to me before Sherman came down !"

The blacks are wearing their new life as well as could be expected. They are poorly paid for labor—and are really incapable of earning as much as our northern workmen.

As I move about here amid the wreck of society, and review the history of the last forty-five years in connexion with it, I am amazed, and humbled, and exalted, in view of the magnitude of God's work among this people. They would have preferred a confederacy with slavery, but now, many of them— the noble-minded element—are glad for the return of the old flag.

I can give you no possible idea of the true condition of the poor whites. I am appalled as I view their future ; their *immediate* future. They have no education, no property, no energy, *no brains*, and no *faculty* ; nothing to build a hope upon.

I do not hesitate to say I deeply pity this *whole* people. Had I been situated as they were—as thank God I was not—I should have fought for my fancied rights. It is fearfully hard to be forced to meet the responsibilities that now burden them : for their property was chiefly in slaves, which are gone ; the rest in Confederate bonds, which are worthless ; and their sons and brothers are in the army, or dead—mostly the latter. There is *no* money : the country is devastated by both armies, and the war still goes on.

CHARLESTON, S. C., MARCH 26, 1865. * * * On Thursday I left Savannah by boat, five hours to Hilton Head, and thence eight hours to this city, arriving Friday, p. m., by way of Sumpter, Moultrie, Wagner, Cummings Point, Johnson, Castle Pinkney—and Folly, Morris, James, and Sullivan's Islands, with all their numberless fortifications. Found no hotel open, but on recommendation of a friend, secured a place which is tolerably comfortable. The dock at landing was half covered with blacks and whites. As the boat was making fast. the black guard, gun in hand, called out, "all dem men an boys wats got no ropes in hand *git off de dock*,"—and every soul marched away as promptly as though a bayonet had been pointed at his back. The only apparent difference between him and his predecessor, who might have been there months ago, was a difference of color. What a revolution !

The city is desolated. Streets are deserted—docks are decaying—entire blocks burned, with nothing standing but the chimneys—acres of houses riddled in roof and wall—doors smashed in, and ajar—churches bayoneted with balls, which, in pushing through, carried away pulpit, pew, and organ—church burying yards ploughed up with burrowing shell—monuments crushed —street pavements in disorder—wide-spread ruin everywhere.

The house in which I write is pierced through and through with shell. The church which I this morning attended was rent in pulpit and spire by the same. Many years must pass before all this wreck can be restored. Many of the old families have retired to the country—the rich are still at the North, though slowly coming back. Most of those who entered the rebel army are dead. Guerilla warfare throughout the interior is a terrible scourge. An acquaintance of mine left here last week for Columbia, to get his family whom he took there for safety before the evacuation. Day before yesterday his body was found on a tree thirty or forty miles above here, hung by guerillas. This is only one instance of their frightful cruelties. * * * I am nearly six miles from Fort Wagner, yet the glass of my windows is smashed by repeated concussions. Within sight of my position as I write, are three rooms *in one* with floor and ceiling free in each direction, made so by a shell thrown first through a wall six to eight inches thick, and then through a chimney. Just ten feet farther off another messenger lies undischarged, of weight about fifty pounds, which, in reaching its resting-place, passed through two roofs and one twelve inch brick wall, leaving things loose all about. * * *

The government yesterday placed at my disposal a boat's crew of seven men, and at my leisure I went down first to Wagner, and stood overlooking the spot where three thousand of our noble fellows tested the love for country by yielding their heart's blood ; stood on the spot where the 54th Massachusetts colored regiment so defiantly proved that black blood will not quail ; saw where, for weeks, our men mined, sapped, paralleled, and finally overcame. Then I went to Cummings

Point, alias Putnam, alias Gregg, and stood by the guns which with those of Wagner and the gun-boats, dealt out iron vengeance on Sumpter and this doomed city, all the while thinking that upon the ground on which I was standing was fired the first gun at Sumpter. Then above the roar of cannon I seemed to hear the echo of four million voices answering, "It is finished." Thence across to Sumpter—a wreck now, as is the system which attacked it, but still in strength omnipotent, as is the hand of Him who guided the storm to the redemption of the nation,—for its walls would to-day successfully stand the battering of three navies. Gibraltar is not stronger! Then across the channel to Moultrie—the men all keeping aft for fear of torpedoes. We were obliged to land a half mile above the fort. The old dock and entrance had been destroyed and closed up by our shell. From the site of the old flag-staff, the pathway of Anderson and his men could almost be seen on the face of the waters, as in that dark, memorable night they silently moved across. The walls are torn and scattered and blistered by our shell—but our forces now hold it with a giant hand. I question whether any civilian had entered Moultrie till yesterday The guard repeated to me his orders not to pass any, but when I produced the permit of the commanding general the way was open—and I felt myself on consecrated ground.

On the return trip to New York, soon after leaving port, he discovered a sad-faced gentleman on deck whose acquaintance he made, and whose story of sorrow he soon learned. He was for many years a preacher in Georgia. When the war-call came to his two elder sons they refused to fight against the flag. So the family property was confiscated, and they were all obliged to flee for safety. They hoped to secure refuge at the North — but in passing the rebel lines to reach port they barely escaped alive — and were entirely stripped of supplies for future necessities, with scanty clothing for present need, and this of the coarsest "homespun" such as the chivalric daughters of the Confederacy had invented to meet the demands of the time. This acquaintance resulted in a generous purse made up by the passengers — and on arrival at dock in New York two carriages took the entire company of refugees to his own residence, where the five ladies and children of this unexpected party of nine were lodged, and all of them hospitably entertained for ten days, — a circle of ladies in the city supplying for them an ample wardrobe; his only regret for this assembly, that having entirely filled his house with *them*, he was obliged to transfer to a friend the privilege of receiving Dr. K., a native Greek, just then arrived from Athens, whose acquaintance he had enjoyed in London, and who sought him on arrival in America.

A stray fragment occurs to mind here which justly belongs to the mosaic of a great and noble life. On the way up the avenue from the steamer, Mr. Hall took his southern friend to the study of the well-known Tabernacle pastor,

to introduce him first on northern soil to that
brave champion of freedom. Comprehending at a
glance the condition, as he cordially took his
hand, Dr. Thompson instantly threw off his
coat and thrust it upon him, saying with tears,
in answer to remonstrance, "take it — take it —
I have another!"

NEW YORK, JANUARY 1, 1866.—In a letter to a friend in Africa he wrote. * * * Since your last date we have, I trust,
emerged from war and strife, into a continuing peace. The
great work of the century *in war* is done—the era of progress
in the nation has commenced. I have abiding faith in the result. I cannot believe God has permitted us to carry through
this contest so effectively, only to leave the two sections in fraternal hatred. I do believe the South will be so reconstructed
that master and slave will hereafter live in pleasant contiguity,
as do the directing and laboring classes at the North.

Just before the final fall of the rebellion, I passed several
weeks in South Carolina and Georgia, and from observation
and inquiry I am satisfied that 33 per cent. of the negro population will die from exposure and neglect before they can be
educated to take care of themselves.

I think the end will give, equally to blacks and whites, right
of trial by jury—of testimony in court—and of franchise : but
the entire work is herculean. Aside from these matters that
belong to statesmen and philanthropists, there is now a work
for christians in this country such as was never before presented
to any nation. *An open way to the hearts of nine millions of
people.* "Have we not all one Father? Hath not one God
created us?" God is calling loudly to the churches. "Love
thy neighbor as thyself!" "Remember them that are in
bonds, as bound with them ; and them which suffer adversity
as being yourselves also in the body." "Take counsel—execute
judgment ; make thy shadow as the night in the midst of the
noon-day ; be thou a covert to them from the face of the
Spoiler." "Then shall thy light break forth as the morning,

and thine health shall spring forth speedily." "The Lord shall guide thee continually ; and thou shalt be like a watered garden, and like a spring of water, whose waters fail not."

From this time to the Spring of 1873, Mr. Hall seemed everywhere surcharged with useful service — but in the Spring of 1868, his overtaxed physical strength partially yielded under the long strain to re-adjust financial obligations for which he was not personally responsible ; and from that date to the end, he sustained a brave struggle for life, — not simply *to live*, that he might enjoy home, friends, and the other delights of pre-existence, — but that he might throw himself more and more into the great currents of effort to bless and elevate the world. This aim led him, though still loyal to the church and to the city of his residence, to frequent and sometimes long absences in search of health. In Chester, Nantucket, Hartford, East Windsor, Whately, and Ashfield — of his beloved New England — anxious hearts beckoned him with tender ministries. In each of these homes the data are clear and vivid of the uncertain and sometimes faltering steps of his progress, — but he tarried longest in southern Europe, and in Montreal, in which extremes of temperature he found favoring climatic helps.

153931

During three successive seasons he tested the dry, bracing air of the latter city — and regained by its influence in the spring of 1870, the voice he had lost by exposures at Gibraltar in the spring of 1869.

Not only did the climate of Montreal benefit him, but her markets supplied the richest nutrition for a wasting frame — and the vigorous physique and bon-homie of her people provided a healthy tonic to his spirits. He entered with almost boyish zest into the open air recreations of the Scotch and English residents; and often leaving the society of his warm-hearted American friends, of whom he found a large colony there, — he watched with enthusiasm the local public games, especially at the skating and curling rinks. There he was recognized as an invalid as well as a guest; and the freedom of the reception-room, with its cheerful grate, easy chairs, and current journals, was no more cordially offered than enjoyed between the excitements of the strifes. So absorbed did he become in the skill and muscular force developed in contests for mastery of the *besom* and the *stone*, that he often forgot his dinner-hour, and remained a delighted spectator till approaching darkness warned him to leave.

Walking up Victoria Square one day, a voice behind him called his name, and presently an elderly Scotch gentleman laid a hand on his arm, saying, "we have a matched game at the rink to-day. I think you will enjoy it. Do not fail to come!" He went, and did "enjoy it" thoroughly.

Everywhere during these years of wandering, he entered heart and soul into the great underlying ambitions of his life. Like Jacob, wherever he tarried, he built an altar, and no one could ever doubt on what ground his tent was struck. Although he never loosened his firm hold on the Tabernacle — his first and only church *home* — he used playfully to say he had *five own pastors,* — Mr. Wells in Montreal, Mr. Dingwell in Ashfield, and Mr. Lane in Whately, — besides his well-beloved Drs. Thompson in Berlin, and Taylor in New York. His regard for the Sabbath, as the Lord's day, was reverent, tender, and perpetual. For the thousands of miles he measured from time to time, on three continents, he never in a single instance encroached voluntarily upon holy time. The sight seeing that could not be accomplished on week days was left *unseen*. The short journeys by land or sea, planned by travelling companions for the close of a week, were deferred, for him and his, till the beginning of another. Frequently he lost two or three days from a specific trip, waiting over at hotels, rather than to spend even a morning of the Sabbath to reach a given destination. If he were to begin a journey on Monday morning, everything must be in readiness to take or to leave, with the closing in of Saturday night, and he often emphatically declared he never knew a business enterprise to prosper that was projected or arranged in holy time.

The letters of sympathy and encouragement, or for counsel in emergencies, that poured in upon him during these years, are now a valued testimony. From his different "pastors" and other clergymen — from young men in New York asking his prayers for individuals, or his advice about locating in church relations, or for guidance in study, or in business or social plans—a multitude of various demand and character, — with here and there a brief note from some business acquaintance in the vicinity of his Beaver street office or Produce Exchange, acknowledging the silent force of his pure example as a stimulus to the higher life; and messages without number expressing "the miss and the loss" of his direct influence on organized work in the metropolis. By request of personal friends, who claim a tangible memorial of these closing years, a few extracts from letters within these dates will be given:

NOVEMBER 26, 1866.—His pastor, absent for a year in Europe, wrote from Berlin: "Your welcome budget of church news greatly cheered me with respect to the prospect of spiritual good for the winter. All the arrangements for bringing the young men together under the best social, moral, and religious influence, seem to me admirably conceived,—and they will surely promote not only the spiritual welfare of the young men who are more immediately reached by them, but also the development of church piety and of missionary activity. The fervor of the young men will be felt in our church prayer-meeting; their enthusiasm will impart itself to all our benevolent enterprises. A body of young men so trained, will be in after years most reliable supporters of the church; and thus we shall escape the fate which has overtaken so many churches, that when their originators have passed away, there have been no successors of like views and spirit to carry forward the organization and its work. This has been one reason for the failure of free-church movements and mission-church movements in New York. The spirit of liberal devotion which planned them has not perpetuated itself by means of a corps of young men similarly trained. But now I see in these movements among young men an illustration of the reproductive power of a good example, through you and others who were so kindly cared for by Dea. Pitts when you were young strangers in New York. His life is living itself over in you; and so your lives will reproduce themselves in others ; and this spirit of earnest, thoughtful, practical devotion to the young will live on from one generation to another. * * * I am delighted to hear of the arrangement for a daily industrial school. This must enlist the co-operation of all who have either time or means to devote to the work of elevating the poor of New York. * * * Love, joy, and peace to you ! Ever faithfully yours,   J. P. T.

AUGUST 23, 1867.—Mr. Hall wrote from New York. What I want—*need—must have*—is a contented spirit, willing to accept what God gives me through my best exertions, as *enough* ; not to chafe because I do not equal my ambitious longings. My stay away has been an immense relief—but the attritions of business life harden me toward spiritual things, and I fall into the mighty current of the eager and unsatisfied, who know no rest. But *wholesome* wealth is the accumulation of savings, rather than the result of rapid and large ingatherings.

SEPTEMBER 15, 1867.—Thursday night the adjourned meeting of young men took place. Everything passed off pleasantly. I hope we shall *pray* this winter as we have never prayed before, and labor *personally* for souls as we never yet have done. Life seems too short to accomplish what I ought, unless I can do more for Christ than I have yet done. Years ago, before I left Ashfield, one of the strongest arguments Satan used, to keep me from openly acknowledging my Master, was the probability that in that case I should feel called to enter the ministry. When at the age of twenty-two I did consecrate the remainder of my life to his work, I did it without mental reservation. At that time I gave myself to a prayerful consideration of the place and calling in which I should serve Him who had done so much for me. I have had no reason to question the decision. On the contrary, I am more and more satisfied that heavenly wisdom guided my choice and purpose. Each passing year has led me to see increasing need of christian *laymen* in a city which, like this, stands as a watch-tower for the nations. Year by year I have felt increasing need of firm, unyielding, aggressive christian effort in New York, among that great class of young men who form the connecting link between the practical, efficient, living power of this city, and the great thinking, producing powers of the world with which, through our merchants, we have association.

This year, more than ever before, I feel that since God did *not* call me into the ministry, He *did* call me to aid in the work of consecrating to Him the pulsating business-heart of New York. I can give myself to Him renewedly, if no more. Perhaps, in addition, I may impart to the mass of young men with whom I am brought daily in contact, something of the Saviour's spirit—if indeed that spirit dwells within me.

I am sure every christian man in this city has a vast field of effort before him, *if he will enter in and work in earnest.*

NEW YORK, SEPTEMBER 7, 1868. * * * We hope you will improve so rapidly that we shall soon see you in New York again, for we young people need your advice and counsel in the prospective work for the winter. * * * In the communion service yesterday we missed you very much. Dr. T. spoke of your enforced absence, and remembered you very tenderly in his prayers. * * * * W. F. B., Sup't Five Points Mission.

SEPTEMBER 30, 1868. * * * The association is formed ! On the Sunday before last, just after receipt of yours of 16th inst., our pastor came into Bible class and proposed a course of lectures to young men, in conversational form, on the evidences of christianity. * * * We were very thankful for your suggestions. Dr. Wm. H. Thomson has offered to instruct us from his abundant stores of antiquarian and biblical knowledge,—and we have work before us.

The association is essentially a working organization, with four committees to report monthly, your name among them,—a mission committee, a social and literary committee, a stranger's committee, and a devotional committee. Dr. T. enters altogether into our plans, and gives us every encouragement. He approves having the church parlors open two or three nights weekly, as proposed : to be furnished with books and current periodicals for the use of young men. I shall write again when we are fully at work, and keep you advised, hoping soon to see you with us. C. L. H.

BIRMINGHAM, ENGLAND, MARCH 29, 1868.—An English business friend wrote : I send you some portion of John Bright's speech upon the Irish church. You know he represents Birmingham in the House of Commons. It is said to be the most brilliant speech ever heard here, by the present generation. I think the connexion of the Irish church with the State must and will be severed : and I think the *domination* of the church of England must follow. You have no State church, and I have no doubt you get on much better without one. * * * I do not think a mixed multitude of men of every shade of opinion, including Infidels, Atheists, Romanists, etc., are the proper legislators for the church of Christ, who declared, "My kingdom is not of this world." I fear, however, that the church and the world so much assimilate that it is become very difficult to draw the line. * * * Do visit us, and your many friends in this country, this year. I hope to see you in the realms above, but I desire again to see you in *this* realm, face to face. I am, my dear brother, very truly yours.

MALAGA, SPAIN, JUNE 4, 1868. * * * My poor father has just died in the bosom of superstition—calling not upon Christ, but upon the Virgin in his last moments,—but God has comforted my heart in the preaching of His word, and in the love of the brethren. My means are short, and I have been obliged to go to Madrid, to serve the foreigners as a guide, where God sent me some proofs of His love and patience. It is happy to see how the Lord is working in Spain ! He has His people here too—and the Saints rejoice to hear of the wonders of the Lord. That little boy—the son of the printer—was so happy to come to our meetings ! He is now in France, in a christian home, where he is being educated. One of our brethren here is in prison. The Lord has shielded me, for the Count de la C. and the Governor came to the house of my friend and asked for me, *but did not find me.* They have *seen* me since, but do not recognize me. So the Lord is protecting. He has His purpose, and His ways are not as the ways of the world. Pray much for us ! Yours lovingly in the Lord Jesus.

NEW YORK, JUNE 20, 1868. * * * One sentence of your letter brought tears of thankfulness to my eyes, "have improved more during last six days," etc. This gave me more satisfaction than *a new degree.* Keep on improving and you shall have the highest title within my gift. See 1 Tim. 3:13. Will it be any satisfaction to *you* to know that you are not *wanted* here—and that the unanimous feeling of the church is that their interests require you to *keep away* as long as possible ! You are continually remembered. May the Lord give you back to us, a new man. Your loving pastor,   J. P. T.

NEW YORK, SEPTEMBER 26, 1868.—My well-beloved. You will be glad to learn that our church work opens most favorably. Appearances were never more hopeful, spiritually. The young men have organized efficiently,—the prayer meeting grows in interest,—and there are several cases of religious awakening. * * * Remembering that two years ago a good deacon so abounded in labors as to make the people forget they ever had a pastor, I am resolved to show them now that they can get along without a deacon—only I spoil it all by telling them everywhere how much *I* miss him, and wish him at my side. May God bless and keep you ! How grateful I am for all you have been to me. * * * You are making so noble a struggle for life that you deserve to have it. I hope you are taking care of yourself, and getting better.

Affectionately yours,   J. P. T.

UNIVERSITY PLACE, SEPTEMBER, 1868.—Dear Dea. H. I take the liberty to write you asking your advice in my personal matters, because I have found that every man I have consulted in your absence has been about as useful to me as an old almanac, or a map of the American colonies would be. * * * I hear your health has improved a little. I pray daily for you. Do not answer this letter, if, in your feebleness, the effort is too great, for we young people cannot live without you, and we are all anxious that you may be fully restored.

Gratefully yours.

IPSWICH, OCTOBER 21, 1868. * * * I congratulate you on thirteen years of unclouded bliss, but I am sorry to hear that your health has not begun to increase, and that you have yet to learn submission and patience. May you pull through, and be good for rich service for many years to come. God be with you ! and guide you to right decisions. * * * But may He leave you until your boys have become accustomed to the dreadful tangle which all who do not die early have to experience. I hope you will find a climate somewhere in the United States to stay in, where you will not be entirely inaccessible to the dear friends who love you so, and miss you everywhere.

How few are as happy in their lives,—in the woof and in the filling,—as yourself. Among all my friends I know of none whose cup is so steadily full to the brim. May the happiness of earth prepare you for more beyond the grave !

AUGUST 18, 1868.—My Dear Brother. It did me good to hear that you are really better. Your suggestions concerning the church fall in admirably with my own train of thought for a sermon upon personal duties. I hope to witness more spiritual life, and more earnest work. Would that I could rely upon all as I can upon you. And yet my dearly-beloved and longed-for, let me urge you not to carry the church too much upon your heart. Your first *duty* is to get thoroughly well, and for this you must drop all care ; even for the spiritual condition of the church. Take time to recruit. We shall want you much next winter, *but we want you more for many years.*   J. P. T.

AUGUST 25, 1868. * * * As to your own case I am disposed to side with the doctors in advising you to keep away from New York. You have had cause for solicitude, but not for despondency—and now that you have weathered the storm you must haul up long enough for repairs. To rest one year and thus to gain ten is a good economy of time. There is no man in all the church of more value to me in my spiritual work,—but your worth to us will be enhanced by your spiritual renovation. * * * So try to be, for a time, supremely selfish.
                                                J. P. T.

NEW YORK, DECEMBER, 1868.—My Dear Brother. A merry Christmas and a Happy New Year to you. Our church Christmas passed off admirably. The two mission schools numbering 640 were bountifully fed in the basement, and had a fine time. They were first assembled in the chapel. One little chap looked through the ventilator and saw the turkeys, and forthwith "spread those glad tidings around," while we were singing of the old-fashioned gospel tidings. After their feast I heard one fellow say, " I couldn't a' stuffed any more." Altogether it was a success. Next Sabbath we shall have a feast. D——, W——, R——, J——, and G——, will consecrate to Christ the dew of their youth. It will be a day of rejoicing. Best of all is the news about yourself. Such a fine voyage ! such a hopeful condition ! We all thank God and take courage.

BIBLE HOUSE, NEW YORK, JANUARY 30, 1869. * * * I cannot reply in full to-day, but would not lose a line of yours. Have tried to make the most of it by public printing and statement, and private circulation. * * * Your very full and interesting letter of 5th inst. was sent me a day or two since by Dr. T. I exceedingly regret the necessity which calls you away from Spain, but we are all very thankful for service so efficient in the start. Is there any one there who can be trusted to carry on your plans ? The whole matter is submitted to you for acting as you think best, or not at all. * * * We have the telegram to-day of the arrest of the Archbishop of Burgos. May the issue between the church and the government be widened. * * * God keep you, dear brother, and give you the health you went to seek. I fervently hope your trip may not have been in vain. Yours affectionately,   J. G. B.

NEW YORK, FEBRUARY 3, 1869. * * * I cannot forbear saying that we are very much gratified with the success you have met, * * * and that we are also very much indebted to Hon. John P. Hale for his efficient aid. It is a great concession for Spain to make. As to the future, we must await the openings of Providence. Please keep on the outlook, and let us know what we can and ought to do. * * * Believe me, my dear sir, yours in christian bonds,   J. H.

BARCELONA, SPAIN, APRIL 18, 1869.—Dear Brother in the Lord. I am glad to hear you have some hopes of receiving Bibles. I shall be glad to receive as many as you can send me. It would be impossible to say how many Bibles and Testaments (filtered into the country) I have sold to Spaniards. As to particular portions of the Word, I could not pretend to say how many thousands. * * * I act according to circumstances, giving or selling as I think best, to glorify my Master. The land is ours, and promise of a rich harvest, as fruit of the Saviour's toil and the martyr's tears. * * * I trust your stay in Spain is to be blest to your body, and strength and comfort to your soul. * * * I thought when I stoutly refused the plan of Dr. T. and —— that I should take a college course of study, that I made a mistake ; but the Hand of the living God was in it. I cannot say, but I often think I should not have been the instrument of bringing so many to the Redeemer's feet, had I followed such a course. God owned my work on board the vessel which brought me to England, and from that time to the present, my ministry has been accepted and owned continually in the conversion of men. "Not unto us, but unto thy name be all the glory." With affectionate love in the Lord Jesus.   GEO. LAWRENCE.

MADRID, SPAIN, OCTOBER 23, 1869. * * * My mind is full of things to tell you—and I am eager to hear of the grand enterprises you have been wringing out of slow processes. Thank you for everything—and hope you will not get weary. Labor for Spain ! fight for her,—pray for her old flinty *sierras*, her wide *despoblados*, her swarthy people who are so ignorant, and yet whom we both love so well. There is gold in Spain,—not of the kind that makes *Isabelinos*, but of that treasure that neither moth nor rust doth corrupt. Let us dig at this old mine till the *Seréno* with his pole and lanthorn cries out our final hour as the night speeds on. We are nothing—we shall fall, and others will arise to take our places, but the cause is enduring " till the trump shall sound, and we be raised." Now let me suggest a few things, and do what you think best. * * * Do you know that little hymn, "Work, for the night is coming ?" Let us sing it three times a day. The field is enormous, the interest intense ! I am glad you are so much better. May the Lord be with you. Yours fraternally, etc.

JANUARY 28, 1870. * * * It is rather late in the month to wish you a year of tranquility and health,—strength for every duty, and grace for every trial,—but New Years lasts all January, and I do now wish you every gift bodily, mental and religious, which are needful to bear you up, and carry you through whatever the opening year may have in store for you. Our thoughts rest much upon you.

JANUARY 7, 1873. * * * Were we rich would not I rejoice to send you a souvenir worth the acceptance of a friend off work and on expense—but as that is out of my power, I will not be denied wishing you a heart full of peace and trust in the God you love better than all the world beside—and everything you need in all the next year's journey.

NEW YORK, AUGUST 31, 1870. * * * We all regret exceedingly your prolonged illness, and the trials incident to it, and also that we did not see you when in New York. May it yet please the Master you love and serve to give you many more years of happy, useful work here, and when you are called away, the happiness of dropping your mantle on some one willing and able to carry on all your labors of love—especially the great work of Spanish evangelization. * * * We shall be rejoiced to year from you as often and as long as possible—and wish you all covenant blessings.

Affectionately your brother in Christ.   W. W. R.

TRACT HOUSE, NEW YORK, SEPTEMBER 2, 1870.—Very dear brother. When Mrs. L—— returned she told me of your bodily prostration, and of the operation on the sciatic nerve, which I learned with the deepest interest and anxiety. This prostration of health is a heavy blow. I hope that health and active usefulness for a long period may yet be granted you. —— said you had much to say to me, and only my fear of exhausting you prevented me from going to you at Ashfield. I was indulging strong hopes that you were rallying, and would soon be with us, which I hope still. * * * "Lord, what wilt thou have me to do" is the ever appropriate prayer. If it is to be *suffering* by you or by me, God help us to bear it. If to *die*, may we go joyfully at His bidding. I hope He has a great work yet for you—and may the words of my sainted uncle, Rev. Jeremiah H., as on our knees I last parted with him fifty years ago, be realized,—"God grant that this may be fulfilled in poor me, 'they shall bring forth fruit in old age.'"

Your affectionate brother in Christ,   W. A. H.

NEW YORK, SEPTEMBER, 1870.—My Dear Deacon. I shall always thank God that you have been one of the beacons that the Father has placed in the channel through which I am passing. I will tell you all my plans. * * * Yesterday I declared at the office my intention to leave business. C. promised to come fifty miles to hear my first sermon. He is not a christian. * * * How happy I am! You can appreciate how weak I feel ; but God has called me, and in His strength I shall overcome. I am now and forever yours.

MADRID, NOVEMBER 4, 1870. * * * I hope you have patience to bear it all—and thus come through the fire triumphant, by the grace that is given you. Some are saved "so as by fire," though I do not know why you should have to be so roughly handled. I do pray you may be completely restored— and that soon ; and that you may be led to give yourself to Spain, yet. The schools and Sabbath schools are full and large. * * * Mr. F. wrote to-day from Cordova, and inquired for you with affection. Perhaps you would like to help him. * * Now may God bless and prosper you. I hope that when I next hear you will be strong and in New York.

Yours faithfully.

NEW YORK, SEPTEMBER, 1870. * * * Your touching letter of resignation was read to the church at the communion, and was received with tender sympathy. * * * The tie of affectionate interest will be stronger than ever. The church rejoices to retain you as an officer, but oh, how I miss you as a co-worker. My prayers are for your restoration to health and to us. My thanks to you (as they are often rendered to God,) for all that you have been to me, and to the church.

Your loving pastor.

NEW YORK, JANUARY 16, 1871.—My very kind friend. Thanks for the assurance your letter brings, that we are not forgotten personally, nor left in our work for the Master without your prayers. * * * I bless God to-day that trial has not been withheld from my lot in life,—that I have known what it is, to pray with the sense of personal want, since I began my studies for the ministry—"Give me this day my daily bread,"—but the lessons of experience are perhaps more profitable when recited in the heart, than if written upon paper. * * * The Lord is with us at the dear Tabernacle. Our pastor seems to be upon the mountain, while many of the people are still in the valley,—but we are looking for a fulfillment of Ezekiel, 37:1-10. * * * Be assured, dear sir, we feel your absence deeply. We shall all, old and young, at the Tabernacle, feel like holding a public service of thanksgiving and joy, if the Lord will fulfill our hopes, and bring you back to us in health, next fall. Pray much for us ! With sincere thanks for all your kindness.

Most gratefully yours,   R.

NEW YORK, FEBRUARY, 1869. * * * God give success to your Sabbath School in Iberia. We heard through the papers of your troubles in Malaga, and were rejoiced that God preserved you all through such dangers. Like Paul of old—perhaps on the same ground—you must go through all manner of tribulation ; and it is as true to-day as then, that you wrestle not with flesh and blood, but with principalities and powers, and the rulers of darkness of this world—and *against spiritual wickedness in high places.* We give thanks for your large measure of success in seed-sowing during this interregnum of God's power in Spain. * * * May He spare you many years, and open every door on earth for your success—and the windows of heaven to pour out a blessing too great for you to receive.   Gratefully yours,   C.

BARCELONA, SPAIN, JULY 11, 1871.—An English gentleman visiting Spain, whom he had never known personally, wrote him as follows : My dear brother in Christ. I rejoice to greet you thus with love in the Lord Jesus, who binds together in Himself all His members—all that are quickened and sealed by His spirit and His word. We are all the children of God by faith in Christ Jesus. We have but a little while here—a twelve-hour's-day-life for serving Christ, *and no time to spare.* * * * Soon we shall be forever with the Lord, and shall be thankful to have served Him in our homeward way. Ah ! dear brother, it is foreign country, whatever spot of earth we tread ! *God with us,* makes the bitter, sweet. You are in America, and there the grace of the Lord Jesus Christ is sufficient for you. Brother Lawrence is here in Spain, and I, for a season, am here also. Your work is ours, for we are members one of another—and our work is also yours. At the mercy-seat, "there is no more sea." When you see brother Palmer of Brooklyn, whom I knew and loved in England, inform him that it is well with me, and that my heart is glad for what the Lord hath wrought in Spain. I have been praying for this people more than thirty years. Farewell !
         Yours affectionately in the Lord Jesus.   R. C. C.

NEW YORK, SEPTEMBER, 1871. * * * This day so long desired, so ardently prayed for, has been blessed indeed. * * * Many times in the last few years our communion service has been sympathetic with the beloved deacon far away. God grant that he may be restored to perfect health again. He has

been *most useful to us all.* I pray for grace to follow the example he has so nobly set. God bless him for all the good he has
done me.

BROOKLYN, L. I., JULY 6, 1871. * * * Your letter ex-
tinguishes a hope I cherished that it might be possible for you
to go to Spain and superintend our work there. Whom, then,
can we obtain for the position? I am resolved not to send any
one till we can obtain a man who gives evidence of being the
right man. My ambition for our christian churches is, that we
may be guided to initiate a wise and persistent policy that shall
command the respect and confidence of the best minds, and
promise to touch the springs of action. But to do this, we
must have discreet and patient men. Please take the subject
into consideration, and see if in the fall we may be able to de-
vise some plan that shall promise good for Spain. * * * I
shall be glad at any time to receive suggestions from you, and
hope if you cannot go yourself, you will give me the benefit of
your counsel.   Very truly yours,   W. I. B.

During this season, the "Provisional committee" of clergymen and laymen was convened at
Springfield, who in their deliberations finally directed the work of the American churches in
papal lands through the organized channels of
the American Board. Mr. Hall was at that
time in very feeble bodily condition, at his
summer home in Ashfield, scarcely able to en-
dure the fatigue of a short morning drive, in
an easy carriage — but the summons, "I have
promised that you will go to Springfield, *and
you must.* It is the hour for Spain and Italy.
Go and strike!" fired him with enthusiasm, and
nerved him to the effort. He was there at the

appointed time — and *his stroke was sure.* In a historical discourse delivered at the Broadway Tabernacle, just at the close of his pastorate, Dr. Thompson made this statement :

"It was a brother of this church, converted here, who years ago began that work of colportage which is now filling Spain with the word of God ; and it was the wise, patient, and self-sacrificing labors, and the magnetizing personal influence of a deacon of this church, seconded by a visit of your pastor to Spain, which organized upon sound and efficient principles the work of evangelization in that country, which has now been assumed by the American Board."

In April, 1873, an obituary notice in the Springfield Republican said of him :

"Not only was he instrumental in starting the American Board in its work for nominally christian lands, but the Provisional Committee who met in Springfield wished him to go to Europe and have the general oversight of the work in its inception. But he was unable to do so—and his disease which led him abroad, slowly wore him out."

NEW YORK, MARCH, 1872. * * * I am so sorry you are having your down days. I feel a concern and sympathy for you too tender and delicate, and loyal, and sacred, to be put into words. But *I hope,*—and remember how often *you have come up.* When I saw you last at the lecture-room I took your hand without asking, "how are you ?"—but I thought, "*what a good voice! how like himself he does look!*" I hope *Spain* has not been the drop too much : but every heart has its own "sweet garden or silent wilderness." How often you have helped me to be of good courage, by your great pluck in coming and going, and bearing and doing, and ever more trusting. Help me still, by your love and faith and prayer. * * *

NEW YORK, FEBRUARY, 1872. * * * I look at your bravery, and learn silence and submission. I feel with you, if we can by the grace of God keep our boys pure, it is all we need

ask. * * * *Blessed are the dead !* but I want you to *live*, to
see some of your work here perfected. Help me by all your
faith and patience, and love, and prayer ! * * * We enjoyed
the "wandering deacon," the "itinerating deacon," but let me
tell you we want the *present* deacon with his good judgment,
and right feeling, and christian love, and weighed words.
Every step you take toward complete restoration is full of
cheer to every body else.

When in 1871, physicians commanded Dr.
Thompson to retire from active pastoral service,
the waves of his grief over this great sorrow
and loss seemed almost to overwhelm him. But
to the utmost, he supported the beloved pastor
through the trial of separation from a church
he had so long and so richly served, though he
held him tightly by the hand till the last
thread of the precious bond was severed. Still
holding him *by the heart,* — his first letter to him
after the separation, opened, "born to Jesus
under your ministry, baptised by the spirit under your hand," — he stood ready cordially to
welcome Dr. Taylor into the pastoral office.
First, in his own words, "because we owe it to
Dr. Thompson to give his successor our entire
sympathy and support, — any other course would
be a reflection on the spirit of his ministry," —
but very soon, with deep and abiding love for
his own, and for his work's sake. During the

mouths that followed the fellowship between them was most cordial, affectionate, and unreserved, but it mostly transpired in his sickchamber, which from about this time was the earthly boundary of his horizon.

The occasional brief notes he received from the retired pastor during this last year on earth were also full of tender solicitude and affectionate regard.

BERLIN, JANUARY 11, 1872. * * * In acknowledging your welcome Christmas note I need not assure you how warmly my feelings enter into all your desires concerning the Roman Catholic church in Europe, but for the present, I must let alone all such topics. You ought to write a history of Spain in its religious aspects, and give your views on this momentous question. *Pray do.* Affectionately yours, J. P. T.

BERLIN, SEPTEMBER 29, 1872. * * * Your letter has come on this bright Sunday morning, and my heart is full of love and thankfulness that I have so long known you, and in a spiritual sense *possessed* you : love and gratitude to God for so true a man—an Israelite indeed. * * * How rejoiced I am that God still-spares you to your friends and to the church. I live in the hope of yet seeing you a new man. * * * God bless you in your boys. Some day I shall be able to return to them a fraction of their father's love for your ever grateful friend.
J. P. T.

BERLIN, DECEMBER 10, 1872.—My dear brother. When your letter of Nov. 20 came, for five days I had been thinking of you with a most deep and tender sympathy. * * * Talk of influence ! Where is the man whose life for the past ten years, both active and passive, has preached more eloquently and effectively than yours ! How much you have taught me ! God bless you ! Yours very lovingly and gratefully, J. P. T.

BERLIN, JANUARY, 1873. * * * Let us contemplate the calm and sweet walks where only the true, the noble, the upright, the good, are found. How blessed there to dwell! Knowing that such paths lead only to Him who is the Light, and such companionship shall but expand into the glorious company of "the spirits of the just made perfect." We are travelling by one way. The present halting marks the quicker going. "If you get there before I do —— I'm coming too."

Ever faithfully yours,   J. P. T.

VI.

Work in Spain.

* * * It is what a man *is*, not what he *has*, what he has made *of* himself, and not so much what he has made *for* himself, that marks the true result of his life. * * * It is a maxim among all commercial men that everything that is worth doing at all, is worth doing well. Now if there be anything in prayer at all, there is so much in it, as to deserve the concentration on it, for the time, of our whole souls. If there be nothing in it, then we need not trouble ourlseves about it—we need not go so far as to engage in it in a perfunctory or formal manner. But if there be anything in it,—and with the Bible in our hands we must believe that it is at once the most sacred duty and the most exalted privilege of our lives—then we ought to make it a real thing, by giving ourselves wholly to it.

Rev. Wm. M. Taylor.

"I have felt that terrible calamities are great blessings to the spirit of a man who knows how to suffer. To such a man, a great affliction from God is like a great blast in a quarry ; it throws out great treasures, or it opens the way for great projects. God seems to have selected him—like a piece of second-growth timber—for an important work. It is not every one that can be trusted to suffer greatly.

When in the autumn of 1868 the state of Mr. Hall's health required entire rest from his New York business cares, physicians urged him to try again the climate of southern Europe. The abdication of Queen Isabella just then an-

nounced, and the liberty of conscience proclaimed by the acting Cortez, had turned his
heart more earnestly than ever toward Spain, —
and doubtless more because of his deep sympathies with that newly-liberated people than for
anxiety concerning his precarious physical state,
he sailed in November of that year, for a twelve
months' absence — designing to spend the winter
in Andalusia.

When this decision was known, the American
and Foreign Christian Union, and the Bible and
Tract Societies urged him as his strength would
permit, to organize for them a plan of effort
among the Spaniards, and to secure the introduction and circulation of a christianizing literature.   General Prim's order had just thrilled
both continents, " Spaniards! you may now enter Spain with the Bible under your arm," and
the American societies saw an open door for the
word of God.   But it soon transpired, in Mr.
Hall's own words written from Paris, that
though this was true, " if said Spaniard, or
any protestant should enter Spain with *five* Bibles
under his arm *four of them would be confiscated*,
provided they were of foreign imprint.   The case
summed up, is this :   ' You can teach and

preach Christ without hindrance — unless the permission of the provisional government is changed
— until the election and meeting of the Cortez
in February. Then you must take your chances.
You are equally at liberty to distribute Bibles
and tracts, *but none of foreign imprint except
by special permission of the government.*'"

Mr. Hall's delicate sense of honor which in his
business relations with men held him to broad
margins and strict justice, against as well as for
himself, also saved him, in the greater work to
which his life was given, from narrow plans or
denominational bias. Firm and clear in his at-
tachment to the Congregational form of church
organization, his heart cordially acknowledged the
wide brotherhood of believers, — and in his labors
to throw light on other minds, he drew aside
the draperies of sect, and sought only to win
them to the simple *corner-stone* of christian
faith. His instructions to the evangelists employed by American societies among the Spaniards
were explicit on this point. In his own words :

"We regard the work in Spain as Christ's work ; and in order to accomplish it to His glory, it should be done quietly, and
with a spirit of love toward all ; carefully shunning all affilia-
tion with political parties or factions, or religious controver-
sies which provoke bitterness ; teaching the faith held by evan-

8

gelical churches without seeking to bias any in favor of particular sect or denomination. * * * In the management of the
Echo del Evangelio it is expected and required that it shall be
just what its name purports. The great leading idea in its management must be the presentation of *simple Bible truths.* * *
God's blessing on our work cannot be expected, unless we use
the means He enjoins."

This catholic spirit was a tonic from which, at
first, some of his co-workers recoiled. On his
arrival in Madrid, the agents of the English and
Scotch societies — earnest christian gentlemen —
who were awaiting there an opening on the
northern frontier for religious books that had
been lying in bond, beyond the Pyrenees, for
years, and who were meanwhile doing what they
could to evangelize the people, called on him to
learn his plans for the same result in southern
Spain. They sought also to secure his influence,
and through him the American financial pledges,
into their organized channels of effort. The
interview was cordial, but brief. "Gentlemen,
the field is broad, — let us work each in his
own way. My work in Spain must be to establish a *Christian* church. That is a simple
name, and it covers all the ground. We cannot
teach abstruse doctrines to beginners. They will
find them in God's word when they study it,
and *the Holy Spirit will be their teacher.* You

have kindly advised me that my plans are premature and unwise, but — God willing — I shall follow them."

These plans were — first, a governmental permit for admission of Bibles and other religious helps *through legitimate channels* along the southern frontier; second, immediate establishment of Sunday schools to interest and educate the children; and third, the issue of a weekly paper that should, without political complications, carry truth broadcast over Spain.

The two last mentioned projects were sincerely but *vehemently* opposed by the argument that Spain was not yet ready for such helps, and that all attempts would result in failure. Still the resolute American was firm in his purpose, and the work was promptly begun. His first plan, — to enter books already waiting in bond at Gibraltar, — involved from the first "audience" at Madrid in November, 1868, to the final order received on the Rock in April, 1869, an apparently endless series of pledges and retractions. In this work Mr. Hall was ably and cordially supported by Hon. John P. Hale, — then resident minister from our country to the Spanish Court, and accepted there as the most popular

and influential of all the acting foreign representatives, — who, with his secretary, Mr. Kinsley, faithfully and persistently pressed the claim
through every officer of the Provisional Ministry,
meeting all subterfuge with vigilant front, —
till at last *the order came.*

When, later in Mr. Hale's experience, our
countrymen learned how true it is that " Re-
publics are ungrateful," *he* doubtless recognized
the Spanish colors so deftly wrought by intrigue
into the texture of his " defections," and fully
interpreted *their base significance.* Be that as it
may, one who was eye-witness of his integrity
begs leave, here, to lay a laurel leaf from memory on his quiet grave in New Hampshire.
May his brave life be ever honored in the hearts
of his compatriots.

Hastening from Madrid to Malaga, Mr. Hall
had just completed the necessary arrangements
for opening a Sunday school among the families
of his old friends, who hailed his coming with
reverent joy, when a political insurrection ending
in bombardment of the city, scattered those of
the flock who escaped death, — and Seville became
the second centre of operations of which the
first full-fledged outgrowth was the well-known

Sunday School in the San Bernardo suburb. Here on a bright Sunday morning in February the protestant fathers and mothers brought their children, all of them curious and impatient to know what was to be done. Grey-haired men, and mothers with infants in their arms pressed into the vacant seats, and into all available standing places, while the excited children were "organized" in classes. There were few teachers. In one corner, the earnest American "*Señor*" telling to a group of eager *majors* and *majores* the story of the crucified ; in another, his little son of twelve years explaining the illustrations and scripture texts in the Tract Society primer to a swarm of delighted *Niños ;* along the central seats two Señoras and one Señorita, catching the spirit of the occasion, and imparting it through their dark eyes and beaming faces among the clusters of girls and boys apportioned to their charge ; a native evangelist presiding over all the motley crowd ; with the listening attitude of the assembly, watching every word as if for life while tears of joy rolled down their cheeks, — was a scene to those who witnessed it, never to be forgotten. Then, as hymns were sung, "Happy day," etc — "I lay my sins

on Jesus," etc. — little voices everywhere caught
the sound, and though at the instigation of
the parish priest the doors and windows were
assailed, and a continual din was kept up outside to disturb, and if possible to break up the
meeting, surely never sweeter praises ascended to
the Most High. All united reverently in the
Lord's prayer at opening and at close of the
exercises, — and passing out, the *niños* hastened
along the street to intercept the teachers at a
crossing, to ask how soon they might have another " school " like that — it was too long to
wait till Sunday again — should they sing those
hymns ? — *more* hymns next time ? and that
evening one of the tunes, never before that day
heard in Spain, was whistled under windows nearly two miles from the *Hall of the Christian
Union.*

In Seville, also, early in the month of February, being impatient of mails and other de-
lays, and having made careful estimate of expense, for which he decided to stand personally
responsible in case the American societies de-
clined to endorse the measure, with the same
press employed to print the scripture cards for
the Sunday school, and almost at the same mo-

ment, Mr. Hall established the first protestant paper in Spain, naming it *Echo del Evangelio.* It was a single sheet of infant size, but the still, small voice of this *Echo of the Gospel,* with its scripture texts, and its carefully selected anecdote or narrative, as illustration, soon penetrated into every considerable hamlet throughout the land. It was a weekly issue, edited by a Spaniard, and sent free into every province. This was a bold venture. Many good men trembled for the result, while such leaves of healing were flying abroad, but Mr. Hall had no fears. His great soul was full of light, and he simply *let it shine.* When urged to relax his exhausting endeavors he replied, "what I do must be done quickly, for *my night soon cometh.*" The rapturous eagerness with which a blinded people caught this sound as it *echoed* over their lovely vegas and through their wild mountain passes was sufficient guarantee for further work — and during the spring, encouraged by the success of this undertaking, several religious weeklies or monthlies were established — in Seville — in Madrid — and in other cities, thus filtering the truth into the homes of the masses every whither.

In Rev. Mr. T., chaplain to the English embassy at Seville, he found a firm supporter and sympathizing friend. Their fraternal relations were a cordial to his spirit while on the ground, — and their correspondence after his return to America was source of much christian fellowship and joy.

In a letter written to the New York Observer from Malaga, in December, 1868, Mr. Hall made the following statements.

DECEMBER, 1868.—"Protestants in America have been mistaken in believing that the Bible and religious books could be freely introduced into Spain. It is true that on the flight of the Queen, the *Juntas*, or provisional governments—which correspond in authority to our New York State *County Board of Supervisors*—upon whom devolved the peace of the provinces, declared freedom of the press, of religion, and of worship.

It is also true that the present Provisional Government, on its acceptance of power and the consequent dissolution of the *Juntas*, proclaimed freedom of the press and of meeting. For some reason not known, it has not announced either liberty of worship or religious toleration,—but both are freely enjoyed, and the ministers of the government, as individuals, assert that they shall be permitted through all the future.

But back of the Provisional Government, back of the *Juntas*, back of Queen Isabella, was an old Spanish law which forbade the importation of all books in the Spanish language, *except by special permit*—and during hundreds of years *no permit has been granted.* If books printed in other countries were circulated, they were either smuggled in, or the officers of customs were made blind by doubloons. Hence this law was equivalent to prohibition.

In order to obtain precise information regarding the barriers *to* and opportunities *for* free circulation of evangelical truth, the American societies sent out a special agent, who should also if possible, organize and open channels through which the benevolence of American christians could be made most effectual.

It so happens that no foreign government is so popular in Spain as our own,—that no people are so cordially welcomed as Americans*—and especially that no foreign Embassador has the influence at court, or among the masses, as our own minister, Hon. John P. Hale. To him are American and English christians indebted for the introduction of the Bible into Spain ; for after English, Scotch and French christians—even Lord Shaftsbury, President of the British Bible Society—had appealed to the government in vain,—Mr. Hale, being put in possession of the facts, with his accustomed zeal and without an hour's delay, requested an "audience" on this matter, and within three days received permission for the entry of Bibles, tracts, and school-books in the Spanish language, from America.

It now only remains for christians to improve the opportunity opened to them. Fourteen millions of people are ready and eager to read and listen—the few Spanish protestants and many catholics are equally ready to distribute. It is impossible to know what will be done by the new government which will be inaugurated in February, but those who have best knowledge believe it will not at present venture to close the doors now so hopefully ajar for the entrance of freedom and light."

The permit granted to Mr. Hale at that time was only a verbal pledge, — with assurance of all necessary written forms to be forwarded to Mr. Hall at an early date. But on reaching Malaga, Mr. Hall soon learned that the English evangelists, with hasty zeal, and in violation of

---

* NOTE.—In a book now before me, after naming feast and Saint days for the opening year, there follow a list of celebrated events to be especially observed on their respective anniversaries. First—destruction of the world by a flood. Second—birth of Jesus Christ. Third—discovery of America, and so on.

their promise to await the results of this first
important progressive step, had, as soon as he left
Madrid, pressed their claims upon the government
as prior to the claims of any other country,
communicating, after all other avenues of ap-
proach failed, *directly with the members of the
ministry.* Through some of them the project
was rapidly ventilated among the people, and
petitions began to pour in upon the Cortez to
beware how they endangered the true faith. These
petitions were signed by many hundred names,
— though in one of them, at least, the signatures were mostly in the well-known writing of
a leading Jesuit Father. Although the members
of the ministry recognized this fact, and did
not hesitate to avow it, they were intimidated
by the excitement they had aroused — and *withdrew their verbal pledge.*

Meanwhile Mr. Hall continued a quiet but
steady pressure upon them through Mr. Hale.

MALAGA, DECEMBER, 1868.—Mr. Hall writes : "It cannot
surprise any who have traveled through southern Spain that
the Moors should have classed the country next to their paradise. All that rich scenery or prolific soil could provide were
given them in the start, with a climate unequalled anywhere
in Europe. They added all that art in their age could gather
from the entire known world, and enriched it with skill and
taste which have never been surpassed. Here after the lapse
of centuries of Spanish domination, during which hatred of

the conquered race has sought to obliterate everything Moorish, the glory of their occupation is still revealed.

* * * We have all been in error regarding the number of Spanish protestants. My inquiries and observations thus far satisfy me that two thousand would cover the whole, and leave a margin. The balance of the fourteen millions are by no means all catholics. A large portion of the men are practically atheists—but there is a large body of *inquirers* who are dissatisfied with the power and the teachings of the Holy Church, but who will not leave its shelter till a better way is open to them. The strength of the Established Church here is in the women, who are ignorant and superstitious, and hence are easily influenced by the priests. Driving up from the station at Valladolid, a few days ago, a military officer of high rank entered into conversation with me. Presently I said, "Are you to have a Republic in Spain ?" "No sir ! *no* sir,—we have five times too much catholicism for a successful Republic in my unhappy country. We want protestantism." I added, "and education for the children." "Ah ! yes," he replied, "*and for their mothers.* Nothing can be done here till *they* see light."

MALAGA, DECEMBER, 1868.—Again he writes : * * * Spain is no more fitted for a Republic than Patagonia. All the educated people concede this. The Provisional Government is in some way pledged to a constitutional monarchy—chiefly, perhaps, because under a Republic its members would be cyphers, —perhaps because the priests, whose influence they are obliged to keep in abeyance, desire a Monarchy. Rest assured, Spain will have a King.

Eight years ago I met here Matamoras and others, some of them since sentenced to the galleys, and some through the sufferings of prison life, released to join the great host of martyrs who have received their crowns. There now come daily to my rooms those who, at that time, dared not be seen in conversation with a protestant foreigner—but who then came to me by stealth at night, under pretense of Spanish wares for sale. One has just gone out, a young man, a school teacher, who less than a year ago lay in a loathsome dungeon for the crime of having on his table in his room, a New Testament.

When I now sit with this people in their solemn assemblies—

see their pale faces made sad through suffering—hear their pleading cries, not for vengeance on their persecutors, but for the redemption of these fifteen millions to Christ—I almost doubt whether I am living in the ninth or the nineteenth century.

JANUARY 2, 1869. * * * No books can be printed or used in schools without first having received the sanction of the Archbishop. One lies before me with this "sanction" covering the first page. On the third is the first lesson for children to learn. "1. I believe in God, one and holy. 2. God, one and triune, follows me. 3. Mother of all, the Virgin Mary, thou art my life and my soul." Next follow prayers on the opening and closing of school. This is the sort of food provided for babes from six to twelve years of age.

* * * Poor old Spain is the most pitiable country in Europe. Not five persons in a hundred can read and write, for it has been the policy of the priests through the rulers for generations, to keep the people in darkness. In all this vast country there is not a Sunday School, nor a place of any kind where children can be taught what they ought to know. Only last June the Queen issued a decree that priests alone should be allowed to teach private and family schools throughout the kingdom, and there was a rigid law that *none but priests* should read the Bible. There was also a law that every man, woman and child, above a certain age, *must* go to the confessional once a year—many go twice a week—or to purgatory when they die. At the confessional the priests *now* ask the people if they read the Bible, and if they do, demand the book to be burned. Through this confession-box the priests discover everything that might weaken the Roman Catholic faith.

Twelve years ago, the English Bible Society managed to get ten thousand Bibles printed here. These were sent to the binding room. The women do the book-binding,—and the confessing of sins, too, mostly, for the men are disgusted with the sinful lives of the priests and rarely go to confessional. These unbound Bibles had not been in the room an hour before some of the women employed there hastened to the priest—the priest to the Queen's minister—and then officers entered, took all the books, packed them away in a damp store-house, where they lay eleven years, and many of them decayed and became use-less.

A few days ago a hall was hired of two men, owners, for a protestant meeting—the lease to be signed on the following day. One of these men told his wife of the transaction. She has-tened to the priest, and soon came back declaring that if he leased that building to protestants she should leave him. Of course the man withdrew from the contract. In all these cities it is almost impossible to get buildings for free worship on account of this and kindred opposition. Knowing of their struggles for liberty I enter their places of prayer, Sabbath by Sabbath, with a veneration I might have felt in an assembly of the early martyrs.

MALAGA, DECEMBER, 1868. * * * I am aware that I draw on your credulity when I affirm that unlike the representatives in Fox's book of martyrs, catholics in Spain actually dress like other christians, and carry at times in their hands, something besides red hot pincers and other inquisition fires. They live in houses, and sleep at night. Persons speaking foreign lan-guages, and recognized as protestants, have been known to live among them for weeks without being mnrdered in their beds. Women go about the streets carrying fans instead of instru-ments with which to remove the eyes of heretics. *Greece bends* as much in Malaga and in Madrid, as in Chicago and New York.

Soberly—even in this age, how many there are who forget that underneath all their forms, their worship of images, their vagaries concerning transubstantiation, purgatory, the Virgin, etc., there lies in many hearts the full belief that the blood of Christ alone cleanseth from sin. The church of Rome is an effete growth from a goodly stock. Ignorance and love of power have fostered the worst of vices, and have lent approval to the basest means to support the worst of governments. * * * I am not one of those who believe the church of Rome has no good in it,—nor do I believe, with a multitude, that it is to be crushed out, and supplanted by some special form of denomina-tional orthodoxy. No, the church of Rome will live many gen-erations after your boy and my boys have added their voices to the innumerable company, but she will be shorn of her tem-poral power. This will eliminate her dogmas, in part ; the

Bible, pure and undefiled by man's teachings, must do the rest.
The sooner protestant nations reach the conclusion that the
erring are to be conquered by the same power of love which
the Master used, the sooner will these great catholic nations of
the earth yield to His sway.

* * * The President of the University of M—— said a few
days ago, "Sir, I am astonished that the protestant world do
not take possession of every possible position of influence now
open to them, so that the whole population can be reached
while full freedom is pronounced." Whatever liberty may be
withdrawn with the opening of the new Cortez, there is, in my
opinion, no fear of farther interdiction of the rights of the
press. Should this government become as bitterly anti-protes-
tant as under the old regime, there will be no difficulty in
printing and issuing religious books, *if all is done in Spain.*
The people will no longer submit to that form of mis-govern-
ment. Never was a people more ready to receive the Gospel or
anything else printed and new. In the cars—on the platforms
—in coaches—at hotels—*everywhere*—people are canvassing,
thinking, inquiring. A hundred thousand copies of the Word
of God, and twenty tons of evangelical books and tracts could
easily be sold and set in circulation during the next sixty days,
if in Spain now. How wonderfully advanced are the facilities
for doing this work! On my first visit to this country the only
"through line" of railway, built by English capitalists—extended from Cadiz, via Seville, to Cordova—with a gap of diligence-
ride to Manzanares—and then rail again to Madrid, from
whence to the coast there was a branch road to Alicante, over
which trains were run as occasion demanded. From Madrid to
Valladolid and Burgos, and thence into France, the journey
was slow and tedious by diligence—culminating in the grand
three days pass over a northern spur of the Pyrenees to
Bayonne. Now those mountains are tunnelled and spanned by
engineering of wonderful skill, and lines of railway have
brought into neighborly alliance all the chief cities of the
peninsula.

MALAGA, DECEMBER, 1868. * * * To-day I write in front
of the barricades. The great square is silent, and the one hundred thousand people of Malaga are awaiting results. We do

not anticipate much trouble. Gen. De Rodas will be here to-night with many thousand troops—will have an interview with the city officers, and we hope they will arrange affairs without bloodshed. We have the American Consulate in town, and our war-ship Swatara in the harbor, so, in case of trouble, we shall be protected.

JANUARY 5, 1869. * * * Last Sabbath closed one of the most eventful weeks of my life. We ran a very narrow chance on New Year's day ; shots rolled about us like hail, but *the insurrection is crushed.*

The conditions and results of that insurrection were stated in a private letter to friends in America at the time, and appeared in New York Evening Post of that date :

MALAGA, SPAIN, JANUARY 4, 1869.—The events of the past week will be registered in the history of Andalusia. The fair of the Navidad, or Christmas time, closed on Saturday week. Before the remnants of fruit and stalls had been removed from the Alameda, this work occupying all Saturday night and the morning of Sunday, the volunteer troops of the city assembled for parade. This was the first organized appearance since the proclamation of freedom, in September last, and the movement was doubtless hastened by the recent provincial elections —these throwing the balance in favor of a monarchy ; though the decision of the Cortes, either for monarchy or republic, will not be proclaimed till February.

The military Governor, Mayor, and other city officers—all in favor of a republic—met on the Alameda to review these volunteers, who turned out eight thousand strong, of all classes, from the merchants and artisans of the city to the contrabandistas of the mountains, and were cheered by the populace, who gathered in crowds to witness the display.

Telegrams carried news of this movement to Madrid, and on Monday dispatches were received from the Provisional Cortes that all volunteers must lay down their arms, and that General De Rodas would arrive on Tuesday evening to receive them.

This command was defied, and preparations for resistance were promptly made. Early Tuesday morning, men and boys were busy everywhere carrying ammunition in carts or on their shoulders to the appointed centres of defence ; women also joining in the work, when paving stones were raised for barricades. These barricades interrupted all communication, were one hundred and fifty in number, doubling upon some of the streets, and many of them were formidable. Paving stones and other missiles also filled the upper balconies of some houses, whose occupants favored the republic, and these the valorous women proposed to hurl upon the government troops in case they should effect entrance to the town.

Things looked dark all around. Few ventured on to the Alameda—the only promenade left open, and the place where daily, in other times, the beauty and fashion of Malaga congregate to sun themselves and exchange salutations by the significant language of their mantillas and fans.

Most foreigners had left for Gibraltar or elsewhere, but the few Americans remaining felt themselves protected by our Consulate, and by the additional strength of one of our war ships in the harbor. The Swatara came from Cadiz on the first rumor of trouble here, matters there having become quiet again, and we received every assurance of protection from her gentlemanly commander and officers. Captain Blake himself called upon us, and proved his vigilance over American interests by arranging, several days before the outbreak, for our retreat to the ship whenever it should become dangerous to remain in town. Meanwhile during all of Tuesday, the work of defence went on. Government troops already stationed here, of whom there had been for many weeks an extra force, had secured possession of the railway station, nearly a half mile from the city limits, so that trains could arrive and discharge unmolested. But the bridge over the Guadelmedina (Arabic, River-of-the-city,) which gives the only direct entrance to the town from the north, except by fording, was held by the militia. Here they had planted their heaviest guns, and this they considered their stronghold—their guards pacing back and forth day and night, smoking the inevitable cigarette ; good proof in Spain of conscious strength.

Tuesday night some troops arrived from Cordova, but were quartered near the station. There was much anxiety in town, but no action. Wednesday morning more troops joined these, and with them came General De Rodas.—Still no action. The government troops waited attack from the militia, while the latter, stationed behind their barricades, invited the advance of the former.

Meanwhile all business ceased. No sounds were heard upon our streets except the tramp of men passing from barricade to barricade. Shops and markets were closed ; not even bread could be purchased, and families depended on reserve supplies for food.

One must have experienced the hush of such a silence over a beleagured town to realize our suppressed and almost mechanical action, as we attempted our daily employments within the privacy of our rooms. The impending doom of perhaps thousands pressed on our spirits, and we felt death everywhere.

But the long day closed at last. The warm, genial sun of Andalusia sent his last smile broadly and richly over the western clouds, and then star by star looked out upon the deserted streets, till night was almost another day.—Here and there, through the long hours, we could see, from our windows, men stationed behind trees or in passage ways, or gliding up and down the Alameda, from point to point of watch; and, now and then, their wives and daughters going noiselessly through the night, with beds and other household stuffs lashed to their backs, fleeing from their exposed homes in the upper town, to the retirement of the southern outskirts.

With morning came fresh reports of speedy attack. Various rumors reached us of the advance of General De Rodas's army. No one could tell when ; but, with the American Consulate in sight, and in full view of the flag we love, waving from its windows, we were ready to risk another day at the hotel.

At 2 p. m. of Thursday the first guns were fired ; General De Rodas was advancing on the town !

The front rank reached the river bank at 4. p. m., and there they halted for attack, twelve thousand against eight thousand men. The inmates of our hotel—French, English, Swiss, German, American and Spanish—gathered in groups from hall to

9

hall, and room to room, and the remnant of the day was spent by us in combined and eager observations of the distant contest. The firing of both armies, and the shouts of the excited and undisciplined militia, came rolling down the Alameda in confusion of sounds that quickened the pulse and kindled fire in the eye. At nightfall the volunteers still held the bridge, but their wounded and dead comrades lay strewn about them everywhere.

In a lull of fight, De Rodas demanded unconditional surrender of arms, or bombardment of the town by army and navy at 6 o'clock a. m., of Friday. A new Governor and civil officers having been already appointed in place of those who had sympathized with the rebellion, these terms were accepted by about four of the eight thousand troops holding the town, including their leaders, as they saw further resistance must be unavailing against so heavy odds.

But the desperate element would accept no terms. They would fight it out or die. So at midnight, official notice of bombardment next morning at 6 o'clock was sent to the several consulates and private citizens, but this was not made public by any of them till morning. We heard renewed firing at early dawn, but knew nothing of its dreadful import till the Spanish gun-boats in the harbor began to speak.—These sent shell into and around the iron bridge, making speedy clearance of that special point, though at great sacrifice of life. Many houses were sadly battered, and some entirely demolished.

Officers Hyland and Newell, of the Swatara, risking their lives in the effort, for they were repeatedly under random fire while crossing, came off with a boat and the flag to escort us to the steamer. There was no time to lose. As I stood for a moment in our enclosed balcony, in conversation with Miss J., who will now be able to add another volume of life among the people to "Peasant Life in Germany," and "Cottages Among the Alps," already written by her truthful pen, a bullet whirred past my right temple, shivering the window-glass that showered over my shoulders. Matters were becoming desperate. Those who had deserted barricades fled to the housetops, bursting in doorways where admittance was refused—and here it was win or die, and every man for himself. If they could not conquer an army, they would slay right and left, citizens or soldiers, friend or foe, till the death-shot arrested their aim.

Leaving our trunks to be plundered, or burned, or left unharmed, as the case might prove, and taking such articles as we could carry in our hands, we hastened from the hotel, followed to the court by our fellow-boarders, with best wishes and " con Dios " without stint. At the portal a body of volunteers opposed us, and even leveled their guns at our heads. Pointing to the flag, Surgeon Hyland and Lieutenant Newell informed them we were Americans, when they dropped their guns, lifted their caps, cried " Viva la Republica," and fell in behind us as a guard of honor to the wharf. We felt the peril of such an escort at such a time, and with thanks for their kind intentions, expressed our preference to go alone. They still insisted, and finding our remonstrances were only making us conspicuous—for with every step our company of chivalric defenders increased, as they ran out from every doorway or street corner, to see and hear and understand—we yielded the point, and made the best of our way toward the wharf, where a boat was waiting.

Reaching the open plaza, on the right of which a regiment of government troops held the fort, and on the left, another regiment defended the quay, the volunteers of our company were fired upon by both, receiving also a cross-fire from the garrison on the mole beyond, and for a few moments shot whirred past our heads in every direction, or fell like hail-stones at our feet. There were only three of our party, besides the officers above mentioned, and the sailor who bore the flag, as our fellow-country-women at the hotel preferred to wait for a later boat. This, as the contest thickened, could not be sent. Our volunteers drew up at once, and fired back, which provoked another volley all around, and those who watched us from windows overlooking the plaza saw no hope of escape. But we scattered, moving rapidly on, and an Unseen Hand guided our steps through the danger.—Hastening into the boat, we pushed off as fast as possible, every now and then a shot striking the water near us, or glancing over our heads. Once on board the war-ship we were made welcome and comfortable, and gave thanks from full hearts for this deliverance.—In the haste of flight, one valise was left behind on the wharf—a target for the troops unless, as we believed, it should prove a trophy ; and we had no thought of seeing it again—but in the evening of that day Captain Blake received from the Spanish Admiral, in reply to his protest against the unsoldier-like tactics of the morning, a formal apology for this unintentional insult to the flag, promising justice to the offenders in due season—and closing with a statement, in high Spanish, of the safety of the valuables left behind by the American party. So we lost neither our heads nor our luggage !

All that day and early evening the fight went on, shells crashing through buildings in their merciless aim from the harbor, or from the heights of Gibalfaro, the old Moorish fortification overlooking the town, and shots from troops pouring thick and fast into the privacy of homes. There were many dead and wounded on both sides—some dwellings in smoky ruins, and many others completely dismantled and deserted. During the night the liberals surrendered, except about five hundred of the most desperate, and these fled to the mountains. By mid-day of Saturday those who had retired from the town ventured to return, and at 3 p. m., General De Rodas drew up his well-trained forces, artillery, cavalry and infantry, upon the Alameda, each department in turn passing in review, an immense body of well-trained men. There were bands of music, prancing of war horses, richness and variety of military dress, to remind one of the long past chivalry of Spain—and no equal display has been known upon these streets since the time of Isabella the Catholic. But there was no cheering of the army —the populace took their doom silently. Fathers, sons, and brothers were lying in the stillness of the dead, or writhing in the agonies of the wounded. Mothers, sisters, and helpless children had been murdered in their homes as the infuriated forces burst their way into the town. The following night was one of carnage. The extra troops were quartered everywhere upon the citizens, and the strife of the previous day was re-enacted here and there, among these lesser groups of combatants, in details too shocking to repeat. Exasperated women poured boiling oil from their upper windows upon the soldiers of the victorious army—and their comrades to retaliate, caught the first helpless objects they could seize, and murdered them without a prayer.

Three hundred of the ringleaders in this rebellion were captured, tried, and sentenced to banishment before morning.

At about 3 o'clock a. m., of Sabbath, a new wail of anguish reached our ears. The wives and mothers who had hung about the court-room to receive this sentence upon those whom they held most dear, now came hurrying through the streets, filling the air with their cries—and it was heart rending to see them gather in knots of six or ten to repeat together their mutual story of woe, wring their hands, or throw their arms about in the most frantic manner, and call upon Heaven for help. Their "ä-ays" will echo in my memory forevermore. Then, presently, through their very midst came the tramp of men, a file of soldiers in front, the sentenced men following, and a rear guard close upon their heels ; going thus, without farewells, to the war-ship in the harbor that should take them to Fernado Po.

Few of them will live to get there, and the remainder might better have died like soldiers, than to be scorched alive in their prison-hulk off that sweltering port in the tropics.

I might almost blush to mention our small share in the great and wide spread ruin—but you will be interested to know that our flight was not in vain. From the situation of our rooms at the hotel we were forewarned of danger, and returning to them, we counted nine distinct bullet shots through our windows and heavy wooden casements.

The city is gradually returning to order. Bands play daily on the promenade, and De Rodas's army are doing their best to veil the scenes of the past week, and restore gayety to the thoroughfares—but sad faces meet us everywhere—and they who mourn are more than they who smile.

The effect will be salutary to good government in Spain, though injurious to the *immediate* liberties of the people. Nothing so detrimental to the establishment of a republic, as these outbreaks. A monarchy is now a fixed fact. Pray that it may be a liberal one !

MALAGA, JANUARY 5. * * * Since the insurrection the priests are jubilant. They are evidently gaining influence at

Madrid. Ten days ago the minister of worship issued the following decree : "The church has jurisdiction of her own,
vouchsafed by Jesus Christ to the Apostles, and to the Bishops
their successors, who must exercise it over ecclesiastics and
laymen. As it has been, so it must be. Ecclesiastical courts
must continue hereafter to take cognizance of *all* sacramental
and beneficial causes—of *all* ecclesiastical offences—of *all* suits
relating to marriage, divorce," etc. Whatever other concession
may be withdrawn, that to the *press* will continue, though
possibly with limitations. * * * The catholic religion has a
tremendous hold on the people. Rome will never yield Spain
till forced to do so. She is too valuable to lose. The work here
is more difficult than in Italy on account of the difficulty of
getting printed truth, and of overcoming Spanish pride in their
ancient greatness.

    * * * Nothing is more painful to the eye and heart in
Spain than the wretched influence of the priesthood. Occasionally a revolution, or a change of rulers, has abated their
sway for a brief period, but for centuries they have held almost unlimited power. They are a body of no mean ability,—
trained to the oversight of civil as well as ecclesiastical matters,
and incorporated with them is the almost invincible force of
the great band of Jesuits. Together, they are more than the
central government can withstand, unless supported by the
masses of the people, and I sometimes fear that the recent revolutions will only result in a gradual re-establishment of their
former influence. It is true the masses declared their will when
Isabella abdicated the throne—when the Juntas, without con-
sulting priest or confessional, proclaimed liberty of press, of
speech, and of worship. But in a few weeks the Juntas gave
place to the Provisional Government. Meanwhile the priests
were quietly concentrating their influence on that body, and
the Provisional Government declared "liberty of the press and
of meeting," *and there stopped*. When urged to declare the
same freedom proclaimed by the Juntas, they refused, saying,
" wait for the meeting of the Cortez." The priests, through
the Provisional Government, thus gained their triumph *number
one*.

    In the first flush of acquired power, the Provisional Government proclaimed dissolution and confiscation to government of all monasteries,—long known in Spain as nests of iniquity—abolishment of ecclesiastical courts, and banishment of Jesuits. Last week a decree was issued asserting the jurisdiction of the church over ecclesiastics and laymen, and enacting restoration of ecclesiastical courts, etc. The Jesuits, instead of leaving the country, have dropped their cowls and gowns and are *biding their time.* Thus the priesthood have gained *their second parallel.* Day by day they make progress, by flattery, by offering political aid, but especially through the confessional. By that open door, through the consciences of women, they draw in to themselves the minutest details of protestant effort throughout the country—and their spies are everywhere on the alert. Thus there is great danger that they will eventually sway a majority in the Cortez, and then all these new-born liberties will be crushed by the mighty hand of tyranny.

* * * In my letter of 5th January, I gave you the substance of decree just issued by the government for re-establishment of ecclesiastical courts, etc.—*virtually, reunion of church and state.* Nothing has given such joy to the church. The Bishop of Salamanca, head of the oldest and most important Bishopric of Spain, followed this promulgation with a column of flattering commendations to the minister of Grace and Justice, and the government entire, for action so perfectly in accord with the highest precedents, and every principle of religion and justice. The Bishops of Burgos and Jaen, being next in order,—and others—have followed with other proclamations. These articles are printed in the newspapers from day to day, and have immense circulation. This is not all. There has just been found at Madrid, with the Marquis of V——as President, and others high in rank as chief officers, a "society to protect and defend the united catholic church in Spain." It declares its first object to obtain the names of the people without distinction of sex or age to the following "petition of all Spain : "

" We, the subscribers, pray the constitutional Cortez to pass a decree that the United, True, Roman, Apostolic, Catholic Religion shall continue, and forever be the religion of the Spanish nation, excluding all other worships, and that the enjoyments of all the rights, privileges, and prerogatives of the church according to the law of God, and all the force of the holy laws of said church be perpetually guaranteed."

This petition is to be put in circulation by the parish priest, "in every parish in the kingdom." All the names are to be put upon paper of uniform size, and when all are received at the central office they will be bound together in one or more volumes. After being offered to the Cortez, "the original documents are to be sent to the Vatican at Rome, as an imperishable monument, and a solemn public testimony of our own faith, and of the faith of our fathers—as well as to preserve in living activity our ancient glory, grandeur, and power."

Copies of said petitions will be printed, and the books thus printed will be sent gratuitously to all the public libraries of Spain, and to all Spanish and foreign Bishops and Vicars. You may expect to hear that five millions of names are attached to these petitions. Ask American churches to pray !

MALAGA, JANUARY, 1869. * * * It is difficult to arrive at the numbers here, or in any of the cities, who are openly released from error, because there are as yet no regularly formed churches—neither head nor leader. Here there are two or three hundred—possibly twenty of whom could aid in teaching in Sunday school or day school. At Seville are two to four hundred good men, the best, as a body, in Spain. At Cordova but a few, with no organization yet. At Cadiz the same condition of things. At Grenada, one to three hundred. At Madrid, probably more. Of all these, not one hundred are now fitted to act as teachers without constant guidance ; but all are ready to learn, and many will make rapid progress under a wise and patient Bible teacher. Others will make good colporters—but even for this work they need instruction. They have, as a people, no financial thrift. They live contentedly on what opens for the present moment, and are not provident for the future. One of their most familiar maxims teaches, "never to do to-day what can be postponed till to-morrow,"—but it is my growing conviction that the only true way to accomplish the great end, is to force Spaniards to do the aggressive work, even though it does not advance so rapidly, nor so according to accepted principles as we would desire.

MALAGA, FEBRUARY 1, 1869. * * * My last was under date 28th January. I entered last evening a small portion of the three first cases shipped to this port from Gibraltar. The balance were examined by the inspector and myself to-day, at the Custom House—meeting his approval—but an objection being raised by the collector, this balance went in store. During our examination, I could have disposed of every book to employées and others at the Custom House, so eager were they for them. I did scatter many—and to-morrow, Pilgrim's Progress, and various other books will be exposed for sale for the first time in Spain, of course at a nominal price.

I go to Cordova and Seville during the coming week.

CORDOVA, FEBRUARY 3, 1869. * * * I wish I could introduce you in person to this beautiful Saracenic city, which Julius Caesar conquered before the time of Christ, and which still has noble examples of Roman and Moorish architecture. It claims to have had the first paved streets on the Continent, and long before the joy in Bethlehem, it was a centre of wealth and commercial prosperity. The cathedral is a re-baptised mosque, and "covers more ground than any other church in christendom." The interior triple Moorish arches are supported by twelve hundred pillars of porphyry of various colors, collected from Italy, Palestine, and Egypt,—and so arranged as to form perfect vistas from whichever point the beholder traces them. The floor-tiling of the Holy of Holies which, strange to say, remains as the Moors left it, is almost equal to Florentine mosaic, and around the sides, and on the façade are Byzantine mosaics of exquisite delicacy and beauty. These were sent from Constantinople when the mosque was built, during the acme of mosaic art. Two years ago the Emperor of Morocco, while here on a visit, wept aloud as he prostrated himself and completed the *sacred seven times* around this magnificent shrine of his Fathers. The famed Court of Oranges, within the cathedral quadrangle, covers an area of 430 feet by 200 feet. The trees, both orange and palm, were planted in 937, A. D.,—but only two of the ancient palms are left. Walking through these streets one needs no Father Agapida to tell him stories of the former greatness. On every hand there are evidences of the ancient power and splendor of the Saracens. Abul Wallid,

Boabdil, Ibul Ahmar, walk with the traveler, as vitalized actors in the great drama of Moorish occupation. Even the legends of Irving become tame before the sight of the eyes.

The son of Christopher Columbus lived and died here, leaving to the city his father's library, and funds to establish a Bibliothique. In the Columbus archives may now be seen the "Tractatus de Imagine Mundi," which contains all the information Ptolemy, Pliny, and others, had gained of the form of the world, copied by Columbus, with also a manuscript tract written by him *to satisfy the Inquisition*, and to prove that his discovery of America *was predicted in the Scriptures*.

* * * There is a vast amount of circumlocution at Madrid on the part of the Provisional Government. Last week fifteen thousand women presented Serano a petition "that catholic unity may be preserved, *and the worship of strange gods not allowed*." He replied that the government had decided not to take action on any religious questions. All would be left to the Cortez. We are now working through all the channels open to us—and the great work daily and obviously advances. Cheerful givers in the United States would have dropped far more tears of joy than they ever dropped dollars on the collection plate, could they have been present at the opening of the two cases of books at Malaga, on Monday last.

Here is a government which with ten thousand trumpets has heralded to the world *freedom of opinion and declaration* on civil and religious matters, but it has refrained from even whispering that no duplicates of religious literature will be allowed to cross the frontier ; and it neglected to say what it very well knew, that without these helps there are not a hundred men in the wide world fitly empowered to teach *the truth* to the people. I fear American christians will debate the matter of printing Spanish religious books *in Spain*, till this door, so slightly open, will be shut again—and then we shall have another opportunity *to fold our hands and wait God's providential opening*. For want of other printed matter, and while waiting the slow action of the government, I have decided to issue a weekly paper—and a Spanish evangelist will soon begin the work at Seville under my own eye.

CORDOVA, FEBRUARY, 1869. * * * Yesterday the priest of

one of the larger churches here declared in the course of his sermon,—supposedly for my benefit, as he had privately set a price on my head—that he wished every protestant, and every protestant book in Spain could be burned—and if he could, he would rejoice to light the fires himself.

The Archbishop of Cordova has just issued a decree that all Bibles, books, and tracts not approved by catholic authorities must be delivered at once to the parish priests, or the holders will be subject to "pains and penalties." The people well know the dreadful import of that threat—and some who are not brave enough to meet inquisition tortures, delivered up their books—and last evening they were actually burned in the public square, the priests officiating 'at the holocaust. The church of Rome dies hard. But if she could only know it, these fires kindle desire for more knowledge—and for every book she burns, twenty will be read.

VALLADOLID, FEBRUARY, 1869. * * * The revolution has worked a marked change in the people, everywhere. Eight years ago there was a Spanish shrug, and a significant silence when matters of government or religion were introduced. Now men are ready to talk freely, and enjoy discussion. But I do feel that great wisdom is needed in dealing with their religion. Centuries of blind devotion to the Papal power cannot be overcome in one generation. In the estimation of a Spaniard, all that is worthy of honor to a nation has been won by Spain's most catholic sovereigns. I am convinced that Spaniards should be employed to preach and teach, and to scatter the truth. Our fathers would not have permitted Englishmen to sell "church" tracts at the doors of Harvard—nor would our brothers of '63 have accepted British phillipics on American liberty at Yale or Union—and I think foreign evangelists who come to Spain and sell tracts and gospels on street-corners, or to students at the doors of universities, *make a great mistake*, for they rouse antagonism, and hinder progress. While we deluge Spain with the word of God, which alone for a while must be their teacher, let us do it effectively and thoroughly, but *quietly, through Spaniards*, and as soon as possible *through Spanish presses*. Through Spanish presses, first, because a hundred fold more readily received ; and second, because far less expensive.   Meanwhile, for the first need of these waiting thousands, send on a good supply of Bibles, primary books for education of children, hymn-books, and other religious helps.

If I had assurance of health, I should not wait twenty-four hours before completing contracts which would give Spain the Bible *printed here*.   Let the people have the Divine message from their own presses, and let them pay for it, no matter how little they give ; for though the priests can easily get away from them what costs them nothing—from the feeling that they can easily get more,—they may be defied to seize and burn books for which they have paid even the value of two cents.

MADRID, FEBRUARY, 1869.   * * *   Occasionally a priest exhibits the old spirit of supreme dictation, but as a rule, they make no outward sign of present defeat.   In this city a few days ago, a priest approached one of his old parishioners, an old man, and still a good catholic, who was selling in the great public square the tract " Andrew Dunn," a Spanish re-print of the American Tract Society, of which the people are very fond.   " What is this ?   Are you selling *these ?* " said the priest.   " Yes."   " You must stop it at once."   " I shall not," replied the old man, " I have a right to sell them where I please."   The enraged priest, pushing him down, cried out, " Be off—you and your heretic books ; never dare to offer them again."   The old man stood upon his feet again—looked the padrè squarely in the face, and coolly replied, " the day is past when you have power to control me.   I shall *not* leave—and *I shall sell these books.*"   The defeated priest hastened off, muttering maledictions.

Here is another instance.   Our old friend N—— went two weeks since to visit two men who were converted at Majorca, under the influence of that earnest christian and unsparing worker, Mr. G.—an Englishman, who has long labored there, and in Spain.   These men had removed to a town some fifty miles below Madrid—and when he arrived, they desired him to speak to the people.   So he went with them to the Casino where, in every city, all Spain gathers " to hear every new thing," and addressed a crowd of eager citizens.   Next morning, he received a note from the eldest priest, complaining a-la Stubbs, that he had come into his parish to teach his people on matters of religion ; and to refute his doctrines he demanded a public meeting that evening, at which he must be present to be heard—and to be reprimanded, if found guilty. The summons was accepted. The evening brought the populace together. The Mayor presided. The twenty-eight priests, which the spiritual requirements of the two thousand souls in that town made necessary, were present, and seated around a table as his accusers. He sat alone, at another table. The house was packed to its utmost capacity. · The priests demanded of this recreant son a statement of his faith. He gave it simply, and concisely. They agreed with him. But when he added, "I do *not* believe in transubstantiation, purgatory, worship of images, or of saints, immaculate conception of the Virgin, or the Pope," their rage knew no bounds. All together they began a violent attack in words, to which the accused replied as well as he could in the confusion made by the sympathetic applause of the audience, and the babel of the padrès. *For two and a half hours* this state of things went on,—the priests waxing more and more furious, till finally they made a general rush upon him, one of them with a drawn poignard, to administer the threatened "reprimand," Fortunately, a brave friend struck aside the lifted arm, in time to save the weapon from plunging into the victim's heart. Then the Mayor assumed *his* authority, and ordered the military present to shoot the first man, *priest or citizen*, who should attempt blood-shed. The twenty-eight priests withdrew from the scene, and the populace escorted their hero in triumph to the train, which left at eleven, p. m. If we had the working spiritual power of the Tabernacle Bible-class-men in as many Spanish bodies, *for one year* in Spain, what a great and noble work might be accomplished. One of that Bible-class, George Lawrence, has been for years a marvellous power among that people.

CORDOVA, FEBRUARY, 1869. * * * Marked changes are constantly appearing in the moral horizon of this country. The past five months have given the people opportunity to think, and freedom to express their thoughts. Men are everywhere eager for knowledge. There is bitter hatred toward the priests, for true to precedent, they yield nothing. Señor S—— a Spaniard, is addressing large audiences here. Many are unable to get within reach of his voice. He has openly, through

the press, challenged the priests to public discussion, but they
refuse. * * * Knots of twenties and fifties crowded around
me, an hour since, to take my hand as I passed along the streets,
to wish me *con Dios*. I leave this evening for Seville. * * *
The spirit of the living God is working among the masses ; and
though churches are not yet organized, nor Sabbath Schools
established, and everything is in a sense chaotic, order will
come out of it all, in time. * * * Seville is by far the most
advanced centre of christian intelligence, as well as in open expression of christian faith.

SEVILLE, FEBRUARY 8. * * * We came to this city just
before Carnival, not that the festivities were the load-stone.
Nowhere have the church or the people, *this* year, indulged the
usual frivolities of the occasion. In times past the cities of
Andalusia have far exceeded the Corso at Rome, in the gay
splendors of the pageant. Years ago, in Malaga, we saw many
hundreds in costume, and the entire city went mad with their
frolic. Bacchus and his attendants in a grand triumphal car,
wearing bottle shaped hats, each labelled with the different
native wines, showered bon-bons over the crowd, as they gal-
loped around the Alameda. Animals, wild and domestic,
prowled around among the carriages of the nobility, or with
leaps of agility perched themselves upon them, as they dashed
by, with their occupants in rich and ancient costumes—many
scattered among the crowds, wore provincial dress, and dominoes,—Andalusian, Castilian, Valencian, Catalonian,—Seville
flower-girls,—richly dressed hidalgos,—Kings in armor, and
Knights in velvet and gold. Conspicuous among these were
Don Quixote and Sancho Panza. Among the disguises,—
zouaves, French soldiers, English "mi-lord and mi-lady,"
South American natives, South Sea Islanders—with goat skins
about their loins, and huge rings in their ears and noses—demons
and fairies,—Negroes and Moors,—clowns and monks,—priests
and sisters of charity,—Turks, Greeks, Italians, Dutch, Scotch,
—everything earthly, and many things unearthly. One chief
Satan with horns and hoofs, attended by a dozen satellites,
made fine acting among the crowd.

Yesterday was Sunday, and the opening of the feast, when
the populace are accustomed to assemble in great numbers in

mask and domino, to dance and frolic on the public squares ; but the excess of merriment enters the church, and choir-boys dressed en-masquerade, in satin tights and slippers, with toga and broad sash of scarlet and white, dance before the Host in the Cathedral, at the close of Mass, to express the clerical hilarity at this juncture in the canonical year. Yesterday, however, though the choir-boys did their duty, the body of respectable citizens refrained from demonstrations on the streets. Now and then a cavalier in domino of sombre black, or ghostly white, passed on horseback around the drive-way of the Plaza, exchanging salutations with richly dressed Señoritas and dignified Señoras in the carriages of the nobility, but most of the disguises, though grotesque and telling, shielded only the lower classes. But from these the fashionable follies of the time received their share of cutting rebuke, and among the caricatures none were more ridiculous than a tall, gaunt representative of the *grecian bend*. The religious liberty of the people expressed itself in an immense figure towering over the crowds, representing the Pope extending his hands in blessing, —and their political independence, in a grotesque figure astride a donkey, and holding in one hand a crown toward a crowd of aspirants, who were jostling each other, and struggling to reach it—each representing a faction,—and especially conspicuous among them, a caricature of Duc de Montpensier, whose futile but desperate efforts excited much intense enthusiasm. Our windows overlook the Plaza where all this was going on— and crowds of clownish costumes gathered every now and then underneath them, to solicit *dinero* of passers by.

I said this morning to a wide awake Republican, "Very meagre carnival in Seville, yesterday." "Ah, yes—*poco, poco,*" but added with an air of gravity, "what else could you expect *this* year, in Spain, Señor ? Too much trouble in my country. Too many sons, and brothers and fathers, killed in our revolutions. Think of Cadiz, of Valencia, and Barcelona,—think of *Malaga*, Señor ! *Think of Burgos, Señor !*" "But there are no processions, this year." "Ah ! Señor—processions are done in Spain. Other years, much processions every feast time— but never again, no, no. The priests must have much money for processions—but the priests cannot get our money now.

All the money we can spare we send to Madrid to support the government. Last September wé had liberty ! and ever since, men speak in some places, and other men print papers for us to read. The priests spoiled our Queen, and they have kept our people poor and dark, but now, *no more of that*. There is liberty in my country now ! we love the church, *but we hate the priests*." "But the priests still have power with the women of your country." "Yes, in many places, but in Seville, *no!* Many, many women in Seville believe the priests are bad, and no more go to confessional. Of course the priests do not like the new things—the papers we read, the people who speak to us and tell us the truth, and open our eyes. They preach against it all. They say to all Spain, in the papers, that we fire guns at the holy image of our Blessed Mary, and do all things that are bad in the church, but the women of Seville know that is not true—and so their eyes are opened to see that the priests are bad You see, Señor, the priests have no more power." I said, "perhaps not in Seville." "Ah, Señor, not in all Spain. The *priests are done in Spain*."

This zealous Republican, in declaring his mind, stated some truths. The priests at this time were outwardly quiet. Only now and then appeared the black gown and beaver on the streets, where formerly they could at any time be numbered by hundreds. But they were diligently working behind the scenes, and they were quite ripe for the darkest deeds, as the horrible butchery at Burgos had just testified. Even while the carnival maskers were parading the streets, the mangled remains of De Castro, their first declared victim, lay in state at the city hall in Seville, en route for Xeres, the birthplace of him who fell before priestly wrath while endeavoring to do his duty as governor of a province. And among those maskers, many of the dominoes disguised the bitterness of a defeated power while they concealed "the assassin's knife." Anonymous letters said to foreign and resident protestant workers, "Beware of the maskers through carnival." Mr. Hall received several such letters, at his hotel, on the Saturday previous, — setting forth the danger to him of going unattended into the streets, entreating him tenderly to remember that a price was laid on his head, and that a plan was ripe for securing it — one of them closing in these words : "Money will buy the assassin's knife — and the assassin's work could never be better done than under cover of the carnival. The priests have their designs. Take care that they are not accomplished." But the soul that was stayed on the Everlasting Arm went alone, to human sight, back and forth to and from the protestant Spanish services of the day, regardless of these warnings — passing, as was inevitable, through the thickest swarms of the populace, in crossing the plaza — and by his very boldness palsying the hands of his bitterest foes. They dared not strike.

10

Late in February, Mr. Hall wrote. For want of other printed matter, we are publishing a weekly religious paper, of which I send you a copy. It is the first protestant paper ever issued in Spain. It is in great demand already, and is warmly endorsed by our Scotch brethren. We know of one soul already led into light by its pages. I have ordered it placed in every reading-room, hotel, and public boarding house. The circulation is rapidly increasing. We hope soon to issue 10,000 copies. N —— is also preaching to audiences of ten to fifteen hundred in the churches in Seville, which the recent revolution has made vacant. His theme "Christ crucified" and the simple, plain doctrines the Master taught. Our bright Republican friend who "hates the priests," but still loves the church and "our Blessed Mary," took from me gratefully a copy, in Spanish, of Bunyan's Pilgrim's Progress, which I brought with me from Malaga—and God grant he may find new light upon his path, before he finishes the simple record of Christian's struggles up to the gates of the Heavenly City.

There are many still nominally in the church, who go daily to the accustomed services, who also attend the protestant services held here, and are ready to be convinced. Of these there are several regular assemblies, numbering many hundreds. One earnest preacher, a converted ecclesiastic, gathers congregations in proscribed parish chapels and convents, and there divides the word with eloquent sincerity. The priests are especially bitter against him, and they have openly threatened to fire one of these places when the people are assembled. The people know that should this threat be executed few if any could escape through the one narrow place of exit—but still they press in, filling every inch of standing space, night after night, and week after week. One evening last week this preacher gave the following illustration of Christ's supremacy in the church : An Irish boy asked his priest—" will the Blessed Virgin take care of me?" " Yes, my son, if you are true to all the requirements of the church she will take care of you." " Are you *sure* she will take care of me ?" " Quite sure, if you do as I command you." " Will she keep my soul, and take me safe to Heaven when I die ?" " Yes, if you die in the bosom of the church." " You are very sure, padre ?" " Yes quite sure."

"Well, I am *not so sure*, for I hear that once on going to Jerusalem she lost her own child, Jesus ; *and if she could lose him, she might lose me.*"

A Spanish mother in the crowd exclaimed, "Yes, yes, *if she could lose her child, she might lose mine!*" and that mother went away weeping, convinced, and believing in *the one only name* by which we may be saved. She has since brought others with her to share her new-found joy.

FEBRUARY 26. * * * The newspaper continues to be, except the Bible, and actual preaching, the strongest messenger of truth we have. I send to-day three hundred copies to Huelva, and the mining regions above, whence loud calls are coming to us for it, and for some one to preach to Spaniards.

Next week we open a regular chapel ; and a week from next Sabbath hope to organize the first Sunday School held in this unhappy country. The outbreaks in Cadiz and Malaga have somewhat delayed our operations, but thank God ! no Spanish Armada can *long* delay the operations of His Spirit. Pray on for Spain !

Nothing here is more interesting to me than the rapid unfolding of mind among this people—since their fetters are broken. Two evenings since, N—— spoke to an audience of nearly a thousand, at one of the clubs. His story was the old one that has melted so many hearts throughout the centuries. When he finished, the President turned to him, his face bathed in tears, and said, "if this is your Jesus he shall be mine !"

Last Sabbath evening, after all who could gain admittance to the room where C—— was earnestly preaching, had stood for more than an hour catching with breathless attention the crumbs of truth divided to them—one said to another as they were passing out, "this place is too small. The whole people should hear the gospel. Let us go to the cathedral—turn out the canons—and gather our assemblies there, where there is room for all." A smile, and a Spanish shrug of the shoulder was the first rejoinder to this impossible proceeding, when an old man in working garb pressed forward and said with commanding emphasis, "if we make the church a God *we have no God.* The gospel may be preached in the fields. We need not seek a large church. *Let us to the Campo.* There, as many as will may come to hear the word of life. God is in the field as well as in the town, and there He will bless us, if we seek Him." Thus is already springing up the good seed sown in tears by the martyr Matamoras and others, who now rest from their labors, *but their works do follow them.*

Señor C—— is doing a great work here. He has in employ, for the Scotch Society, several men who were formerly priests, but who, several years ago, "saw the light." He devotes his entire time to the training of students, and supervision of these active workers. He has applied to me for 6000 copies each, of Bibles and Testaments, as soon as they are entered.

It will interest you to know that the R. C. Archbishop of Seville has just suspended four R. C. Priests for preaching *against* protestantism. The effect of their preaching aroused (by actual count) forty families to a search for the validity of their faith, and the search ended in their coming to the light.

SEVILLE, FEBRUARY, 1869. * * * The interval between the outbreak of the revolution of September last, and the election of a King by the Cortez, now in session, is the period of Spain's largest liberty for years to come, and therefore the period during which most can be done to sow the seed. The inhabitants of southern Spain, and particularly of Andalusia, are more enlightened than the people of the north. They were restive during Isabella's reign—frequently disturbing her life of vice by outbreaks against the government—and now they speak as *men in earnest* when they address the Cortez with a petition that their King may be "none other than the Eternal Author of mind and spirit—God who is in Heaven."

At a meeting of the Republican party in Madrid, February 13, 1869, the member of the Cortez from Cadiz, Emilio Castellar, the "golden-tongued" orator, spoke thus :

Gentlemen : I shall speak briefly, first, because of limited time ; and second, because had I fame as an orator it were not my pleasure to pronounce useless discourses. I must reserve my strength for the great day in which, in another place, we may give pacific and legal battle for the republic—being assured that my presentiments will be fulfilled—my mysterious hope realized—that monarchy is finished in Spain ; that my country wishes no more Kings ; and that we are soon to plant, as an example to Europe, and for the admiration of the world a *Federative Republic*. (Great applause.)

For the present, citizens, there is an affair that pre-occupies us, that ought to pre-occupy us above all other affairs,—and that is *religious liberty*,—for to obtain religious liberty it is necessary to agitate public opinion. But here let me add, to agitate rightly public opinion it is necessary to have what is always needed in advance parties—*prudence*.

Citizens: Here, where I now address you, others before me have spoken on personal questions,—here they have reviewed the past. Let us not remember those who are left behind in the path of progress. There is nothing more worth our consideration than the nation—than the people. There is nothing more powerful than ideas. Those who abandon the people—abandon ideas—abandon themselves. They tread under foot their crown of glory ; and we ought to leave them behind that they may awake to the judgment of their own consciences. (Great applause.)

To treat then, citizens, this question of religious liberty it is necessary to persevere in efforts that our desire may be accomplished ; but it is *not* necessary to provoke tumults by our haste. The Mayor of Madrid has issued an edict that has awakened in our midst certain susceptibilities worthy to be considered, because they prove our unutterable love of liberty. But with candor, I ought to say that night manifestations are always dangerous—and moreover, it is quite suitable that those who defend liberty—who represent the boldness of our progressive ideas, should present ourselves to the open air and to the light of day, in order that the world may see us—and that the people may contemplate our advancing steps. (Applause.)

Yes, citizens, I approve that we protest legally through a commission, against all the limits that might be put to the right of meeting,—but I ask you for many considerations that I cannot here express,—though you make *to-day* a solemn manifestation in favor of religious liberty, do not repeat it *to-night*. By this you will show to the world that you unite wisdom and caution—in uniting the cause of authority with the cause of liberty. Maintain your rights with the greatest respect for public order. Public order is the basis of all liberty—public order is our ensign—public order is our victory. As we have already enjoyed four months of the republic, and hope to enjoy many more, this question of *public order* may come before the Cortez. When we declare to them that we do not need a King to keep public order, that we know how to keep it ourselves, then doubt not our bitterest enemies will gather themselves to the saving idea of a republic. (Applause.)

Citizens : We are to speak now on the question of religious liberty. In all epochs of our history the liberal legislators of Spain have made tremendous concessions to the church—tremendous concessions to the clergy. Remember the most luminous epoch of our history—that of 1808. The legislators of Cadiz began that memorable *democratic constitution*, invoking the Holy Trinity. They followed with the announcement to the world that the Catholic, Apostolic, and Roman religion was the only religion for Spain. They assumed acts of piety so great as to confirm St. James as the patron saint of Spain, notwithstanding he never was *in* Spain,—and to name as his co-patron, Santa Teresa of Avilla ; acts of piety which ought to have secured for them—had the clergy been friendly to public liberty—*a bull to go body and soul to high Heaven*. But what *did* come of it, citizens ? Scarcely had Ferdinand VII assumed the power of the throne when he re-established tribunals of the holy office—rekindled the fires of the inquisition—and the legislators of Cadiz, in spite of all their piety, were persecuted —yes, and would have been roasted in those fires, had not the breath of ideas rolling in upon us *from the fate of four centuries*, extinguished them.

Later, citizens,—in 1820—the struggle was renewed, and the people again agitated the question of religious liberty. In the year 1823, those who, three years before, had dared to agitate public opinion on this subject, *were banished from the country.*

In the year 1836, the constitution was re-formed, and the catholic religion was again declared to be the religion of all Spain. What happened then, gentlemen ? The Friars blessed the troops of a faction that they might use their arms against the heart of the Cortez.

In the year 1854, we put into the constitution the most lamentable article that could be introduced. This article aroused the indignation of the liberal party, and brought upon us the derision of all Europe. It declared that no one could be persecuted for his religious opinions unless they were manifested in public actions *contrary to the dogma*—(or doctrines)—*of the church.* By this, we justified, indirectly, the horrors of the inquisition ; justified them, because neither the inquisition nor the church ever judged *the conscience*, but *external actions.* This second basis which, indeed, was a revolution against all the principles of liberty, was near producing civil war in our midst—and *did* restore again the arms into the hands of a faction.

The Carlists and the clergy are united and indissoluble in their external errors. For *this* reason our present revolution began on the question of religious liberty—on the question of right to plant liberty of worship. Why was this, citizens ? Because we are convinced that all liberties mean nothing,—that it is of no avail to move the hands or the feet,—to feel the heart beating with life,—if the great motive does not actuate us,—*if conscience is not free ;* because, the conscience is to our life *what steam is to the locomotive !* (Tremendous applause.)

Citizens : In this great religious question, let us have no conference with the clergy, because, absolutely speaking, we *cannot* have it.

In 1847, Pius IX ascended the pontifical throne. His hands, which held the signs of religion, allowed the light of liberty to escape. The nations went down on their knees in the dust. The great thinkers—the strong minds of the people, *went to the confessional.* Garibaldi returned from America believing that Italy would be free—raising itself like a Greek statue upon christian altars,—and immediately the Jesuits *threatened* Pius IX. They converted him to *absolutism*, telling him that their party was the essence of his doctrine. And now the Pontiff-King sustains the execrable gibbet,—elects for his prime minister *the executioner* who shows to the world his hands crimsoned with human blood,—and appears upon the infamous scaffold, not as the heir of Christ, but as the heir of Nero or Heliogabalus. (Great applause.)

In view of all this antagonism of the official priest-hood, what shall we do for our liberties ? Are we to ask the government to *decree* liberty of worship? (Cries of yes, yes.) Well, I say *no*. Liberty of worship is not to be sought as a favor. It is to be *taken* as a *right*. (Prolonged applause.) We ought not to ask this government nor any *human* power for the liberty of our conscience. Our conscience belongs to *us*—because it is the sacred property of our individual souls—the indestructible basis and eternal crown of personality ; and any government, any assembly, any King, that may dare to put hands on our conscience *is a traitor*, and only deserves a rebellion at our hands, because the right of rebellion is sacred when it is employed in defending the holiness of our belief, the faith of our souls. (Great applause.)

Citizens : Neither the government, nor the Cortez, nor the whole nation, can interfere with our conscience. No one has a right to regulate for us, our conscience. Individual rights are by nature illegislatable, and consequently there is *no* assembly, nor any power that has control over individual rights.

The church, and her great host of Jesuits, pretend to be the only depositaries of the truth, and consequently sustain the infamous theory that they can use even murder against the enemies of their *holy* catholic faith. Do you not remember how Rome blessed the murderers who sharpened their poignards against William the Silent, Coligny, and Elizabeth of England?

I have seen the palace of the Pope. I have visited what they call the Kingly Hall. It is the threshold over which all the families of the world go, on their knees, to ask a relic and a blessing, and to leave there in exchange—*some money*. Do you know what there is in the galleries of the Vatican? I will tell you—not from report, but from what my own eyes have seen —the donation of Constantine, *i. e.*, the temporal power of His Holiness painted there, *and it is a lie*. Charlemagne, one of the greatest supporters of the Pope's temporal power, and consequently one of the greatest curses of the world, is painted there. There too, is Ferdinand V, the catholic—I do not know for what reason—whether for having discovered America, or for having founded the inquisition ; and there, citizens, in the Salon that leads to the rooms of the *Dispenser of Morality*, the *chief of all religion*—there are, crowned by angels, placed as in apotheosis among the glories of the church, *the murderers*

of Coligny; the infamous men who crimsoned with blood the
river Seine, in the massacre of St. Bartholomew. So that the
Popes have sanctified murder ! have blessed crime ! We ought
not to be astonished, therefore, when we see that if the civil
authority interferes with property on what they call religious
authority, they appeal to murder : and that infamous act
against the government of Burgos is committed—so infamous
that it is asking justice from Heaven—and justice will be done,
because in this innocent blood the enemies of the country and
of liberty *are drowned.* (Great applause.)

Now, then, gentlemen, it is not convenient, absolutely, to ask
liberty of worship of the government ; but it *is* convenient to
say that we *will have it,*—and then we shall *keep it.* This it is
convenient to say, that we shall never allow our conscience to
be plundered. Whether you may be Catholic, or Rationalist,
or Protestant, or Jew,—Materialist or Idealist,—is it not time
for you all to be resolved—and to raise hands to Heaven and
say that there is no jurisdiction on the earth, upon the property
of your souls ? (Cries of yes, yes.)

What does a government, as a provisional government, deserve, which having had in its hands the cosmic matter during
four months to make a new world, has only taken care to make
a new King ? It deserves that we cast it into oblivion.
(Applause.) Individual rights are illegislatable. The relations between the Church and State are illegislatable. We ought to ask
from the Cortez, who are the representation of the country—the
product of universal vote,—the radical and complete separation
of Church and State. (Cries of well, well.) Individual rights,
I repeat, cannot be legislated. Relations between Church and
State cannot be legislated. Consequently, when the Cortez
legislate, you ought to say that you are not ready to give a
farthing to the priests, because they do not know how to pre-
vent murder when the magistrates* of the country visit the
churches to protect the property of the State. I know very
well that they say the separation of Church and State does not
exist in England, or Switzerland, or Prussia. It only exists in
America. And many may ask me, why do you wish to establish it in Spain ? I believe, citizens, that Spain is the country

* Alluding to the assassination of De Castro, at Burgos.

pre-destined in the great plan of Providence to exercise all reforms. Our want of industry is a very sad fact—so is our want of agriculture—of riches. We are a country almost un-inhabited. This condition is caused by *intolerance*. But we have an advantage, citizens, to which I call your attention,— and that is, that we have very strong muscles,—that we have a large country in which to accomplish what civilization de-mands of us. (Cries of hear, hear.)

Besides, we are a valorous race. We have proved this valor fighting seven centuries against the Arabs,—discovering an un-known world in the solitude of the Atlantic,—and uprooting the sceptre of Napoleon on the Pyrenees. Well then, we can show our moral valor by defending this basis of civilization, this basis of our liberty,—*separation of Church and State*. Then a new epoch of our history will begin.

And so, as you Spaniards, were the heroes who at the dawn of the Middle Ages discovered America, the new material world,—you will be to-day the heroes, who at the beginning of the Modern Ages, will discover a republic, the new moral world—where all the races will take shelter as an inviolable asylum,—where we shall permit only *one* King, and that King will be the Eternal Author of nature and spirit—God who is in Heaven ! (Tremendous applause.)

SEVILLE, MARCH 2, 1869. * * * Last night we dedicated the " First Christian Union Chapel of Seville," in Barrio San Bernardo.   The building stands on almost the precise spot made sacred in the days of the inquisition, by the blood of martyrs, the *Autos de Fe* of Seville. Señor V——, now seventy-nine years old, and for seventeen years actively employed in secret dissemination of the truth, and who has many times been obliged to flee from arrest on account of his faith, expressed a wish to be present, as also did Señor C——.   A crowded audience listened to the simple statement of the object for which the building had been secured, viz : "To train ourselves in His service by whom we are all made free," by Sabbath morning services of preaching, by afternoon Sunday school instruction, with religious services on Sabbath and Thursday evenings, and on all other evenings a school for adults.   The Mayor of the Barrio was present, and after the services, examined with interest the Bible lying on the table, and the Scripture cards suspended on the walls,—but the house was made up of hard-working men and women, evidently those who had tasted bitterness, and craved some satisfactory solace. The school will be called, "El Escuela del Evangelio," or School of the Evangelists.

No one can tell what a day may bring forth in political affairs. Some time since I wrote you of a society formed in Madrid to get the signatures of all supporters of the true faith in Spain. The minister of Grace and Justice who has charge in the Cortez of all religious questions, in his report to that body a few days since, said, "These advocates of religious intolerance have sent me one petition on which are *forty-six hundred* names, but all of them in the hand-writing of *four persons*." He also stated that the property of the church was valued at $170,000,000, and now the government had suppressed less than six hundred of the nine hundred convents and monasteries, and in some of these there were no more than five, four, and even *two* occupants. He concluded by saying, "The Roman Catholic clergy have been, from the beginning, the incarnate enemies of liberty in Spain, and they have conspired with arms, and with gold, to cause civil war and to restore the Bourbon government." This looks well for enlarged toleration. May the minds of these rulers be opened wider and wider—and may light from Heaven be poured in upon them till they are filled with true wisdom and *justice* and *grace*. One hundred persons last evening came to be registered as pupils in *Escuela del Evangelio*.

SEVILLE, MARCH 3, 1869. * * * Last Sunday, February 29th, was a day of lasting memories in my calendar. Eight years ago this very season, on the Sunday preceeding "Easter," I stood on the steps of the Seville cathedral, amidst a numberless throng, to witness the pageant of image-procession and image-worship, as Spain only could introduce it. Seven life-size figures of the Virgin Mary, clothed in robes of velvet and satin, embroidered in jewels and gold,—and one of these, the chief idol of the people, the "Mary" of their feasts and fasts, wearing in her wooden ears, and around her dingy neck, $1,000,000 in diamonds alone—were borne through the streets on the shoulders of men, besides no end of Saints and Apostles, with one figure of Christ bearing his cross, as an accessory of the Immaculate Mother. A learned and distinguished professor in an American college, an avowed Romanist, if not a Jesuit, —but whose genial, social courtesies are a fragrant memory— said to me, as we stood side by side, "You see now, a proof, I hope a *convincing* proof, of the beauty of our holy religion. See how the people are *of one mind*. You protestants are divided among yourselves. We are a unit in our faith." Turning my eye full upon him I replied, "Dr. ——, do you believe this people *are* all of one mind? If they might search the Scriptures for light, and liberty to choose for themselves were granted them, I believe multitudes would *to-morrow* refuse homage to these images of wood." "Never, no *never!* Spain will never desert the true church. I do assure you this is *heart* devotion."

Three days ago I stood on the balcony of our rooms, overlooking the Plaza, and saw *six thousand* of this same people pass through the same streets, not with images of the Virgin Mary,—but with banners and mottoes declaring their allegiance to her Son. This year there will be, for the first time in Spain, no Holy Week processions of "our Blessed Mary." The priests dare not attempt the pageant, for fear of riots among the people, the lawless element of whom have loudly threatened disturbance if the farce is undertaken.

The pacific procession, declaring for liberty of conscience, had gathered on the old inquisition ground in San Bernardo quarter, and they disbanded on another site of inquisition fires on Alameda Hercules, at the opposite extremity of the city. The very air was pregnant with the exultant cries of the great host of martyrs, as I read on a passing banner, "Christ has made us free!"

SEVILLE, MARCH 13, 1869. * * * Last Sabbath we organized the first Sunday School in Spain, in the chapel in Barrio San Bernardo. Without the Estrella de Belen, with its hymns and music, and the lesson-books for children, especially the American Tract Society primer, we should have been at great loss. We opened with seventy. If we had a supply of books we could organize twenty more Sunday Schools in as many days. The enduring strength of this work in Spain depends largely on the proper instruction of this generation of children. No pen can describe the manifest pleasure in every movement and response of the assembled children and their parents. They were dressed in their best, and conducted themselves during all the exercises, as well as average Sunday School children in America. At opening and close of the exercises parents and children joined reverently with bowed heads in repeating the Lord's Prayer. The first hymn was sung from the American Tract Society " Estrella," to the tune so familiar at home—" Happy Day," etc. I may be sanguine, but judging from the readiness with which the children took up both hymns and tunes, the day is not far distant when our American Sabbath School songs will be the lullabys of half the nurseries in Spain.

In the evening of that day we heard one of the tunes whistled by a Spanish boy under our windows, nearly two miles from the building where the school is held.

In the San Bernardo building we propose to hold two·public services on each Sabbath, with a Sabbath School in the afternoon,—and during the week training schools for adults, having in view their preparation as Bible-readers in the surrounding towns ; and now, if suitable men could be found, we could put six or eight more into immediate active chapel labor. But the men are not to be obtained. We must first mould them. This is one of the first works ; and for early training of these workers it is very important for your missionary to be soon on the ground. Seville has a population of 125,000 souls—and in my opinion it is to be the centre and bulwark of protestantism in Spain.

SEVILLE, MARCH 17, 1869. * * * Last Sabbath was stormy, but our rooms were filled, early, with all the children of the preceeding Sabbath, and many more. Such as could read were given a copy of St. John's Gospel, from which they studied their lesson for the day. With marvellous facility they learned and sang, " Come to Jesus," in addition to " Happy Day " of the Sabbath before. Representatives from Madrid were present to observe our manner of organization, and to secure, if possible, singing and instruction books for the establishment of a school in that city, but until the permit is received from government, we have none to spare.

The parish priests are using all their powers to intimidate the people, but they can no longer control them. The rooms are crowded, especially for the preaching services, and the streets also are filled as far as the voice of the speaker can be heard.

The *Echo* continues in demand. Last week we issued three thousand copies. Next week's issue will number four thousand. The priests denounce it as the *Echo of Hell*.

Mr. C——'s observations and experience agree with my own, that native pastors and teachers require constant, vigilant, but patient watch, to keep them in the right path. They are tempted not only to attack the church which has so long deceived them, but to harangue the clubs—thus committing themselves, as patriots, to unwise complicity in the political agitations of their country.

All southern Spain is feverish regarding civil government. The present disposition of the Cortez to promote the Duc de Montpensier to the throne is the chief cause of this excitement. *He is a Bourbon*, and he could not be made King without a serious outbreak throughout Andalusia. An intelligent Spaniard said to me a few days since, "If Duc de Montpensier comes to the throne—very well—he will be there *very short time.*" "Why : is he so old ?" "No, no, Señor, but he will be *killed* if he tries to be our King." "Oh, no, not so !" "Si, si, Señor, I speak the truth. There are secret societies organized in every large town in Andalusia. They are pledged by solemn oath to take his life, if he is made King. If one fails, another will try, and they will keep trying till some one succeeds, no matter how many die. Why, Señor, *he is a Bourbon*, and Spain *has had enough of that blood !*"

Said another respectable citizen, "If Montpensier is made King we will fight his rule. *All Andalusia will fight*—and if it comes to that, *the women too !* we will have *no more Bourbons* over us."

No human wisdom can foresee the immediate future of Spain. A bigot on the throne, whatever may be the constitution, will soon be manipulated by the priesthood, who still hold enormous powers through the confessional. Hence we cannot be too active sowing good seed everywhere, that it may come to fruitage now. Doubtless freedom of worship will be guaranteed by the new constitution, but a King, under the control of the church, can make even that article nugatory.

MARCH 20, 1869. * * * The state of my health requires that I leave this climate as soon as possible ; and whenever this long contest is over, and I can secure the proper entry of the cases of books now lying in bond at Gibraltar, I shall hasten to Italy, and thence to Switzerland and Germany for the summer, —but shall take Valencia and Catalonia in my way, crossing a southern spur of the Pyrenees to Perpignan, that I may spend also a little time in Barcelona. I hope to conclude such arrangements here, that hereafter books can enter with only one trans-shipment, via Liverpool.

The weekly issue of the Echo continues, and is now equal to about 75,000 pages of tracts, per week, and each page is worth a dozen tracts, for reasons you can readily understand. I consider it, at present, our most important agency. Its articles have been copied by most of the secular papers, and several of them, in the interior and north, ask for exchange. The distribution is in wise hands,—but the paper meets violent opposition from the priests, which is a good endorsement. A letter just at hand, from one of them in Gallacia, salutes, " the child of Satan who publishes that diabolical sheet, El Echo," etc.

Padre G——, one of the most able canons in the cathedral, has just attacked Señor A——, and Señor C——, calling them opprobrious names, and publishing his letter in a pamphlet for general circulation. It has had extensive sale, but unfortunately for himself it is denounced by his own people. He felt the derision so keenly, that he challenged Señor A—— to an argument before the University of Seville, and the public, presuming he would decline. But Señor A—— promptly accepted the challenge, and poor padre G—— was forced to withdraw, knowing, as he well does, that he could not support the positions he assumed against his antagonist.

I give you these items to show you what advances truth is making. I cannot agree with those who advise delay till there is crystallization here. It is of vital importance *that we give form to the crystals.* This state of the masses requires skilled refiners. The efforts of protestant christians in Spain during the past year have done much to introduce and sustain liberal sentiments in the new constitution of the country ; and this people need constant sympathy and support *from without,* in their future struggles for liberty.

Think of a city in Spain establishing *free public schools.* Seville is doing it !

It is not necessary to explain here all the reasons for a sudden call Mr. Hall received at this time to go to Gibraltar. The parties most interested need no reminder of them. It is quite enough for his many friends, and especially for those who counted his life dearer than their own, that a mis-appropriation by agents of other societies, of the permit for entry of books for which he had toiled so persistently all winter, involved for him exposures on the sea trip to the Rock, prolonged by the easterly winds prevailing there at that season, which resulted in entire loss of voice for ten months. Those exposures have ever been regarded by his family as the fatal crisis in his disease. During that trip he lost more than all the physical gain he had made hitherto, in the long absence from home and country. From that date, the rallying point seemed undermined, — relapse following relapse, till the end. When urgently entreated not to risk his life to undo what should never have been done, and for the doing of which others alone were responsible, he calmly but firmly replied, "If it is my last work on earth I shall get *one* case of these books through the customs, into Spain, though I have to bring them as personal luggage, *and pay their weight in gold.*" A telegram to Mr. Hale at departure from Seville, followed by others in the progress of his trip, secured more than he had dared to believe possible — and he received at Gibraltar, a few days later, a renewal of his permit from the Cortez. So that though he laid down his life in this work, he had the joy of seeing it accomplished.

GIBRALTAR, APRIL 6, 1869. * * * We left Seville a week Monday, going as far as Cadiz by rail, which is land's end in that direction. There we were obliged to remain four days for a steamer, and even then we came to one landing only, at Algeciras, a Spanish town across the Bay—coming to the Rock with our luggage, on a tossing, white capped sea, in a little sail-boat, which seemed determined to empty its cargo, before reaching port. With the wind in our favor we were *one hour and a quarter* in crossing. We shall be detained here fully a week, I fear, at shortest—in these searching winds. The rock is dangerous to invalids at this season of the year. Even the monkeys that inhabit the northeastern front, are driven from their rendezvous, and flee to the sheltered portions, near the lower town, during the prevalence of these winds. I shall get away as soon as I can accomplish the work for which I came.

SEVILLE, APRIL 15, 1869. * * * I wrote from Cadiz, advising you of the terms of the new constitution. I then had only the telegram before me. The full text is not entirely sat-

11

isfactory, but let us hope the debate, now in progress in the Cortez, will change the phraseology of several clauses so as to enlarge the privileges of protestants. The chapel and school are prospering—attendance large in both—and interest unflagging.

I can give you no idea of the wearying details of this pressure on the government for written endorsement of their verbal pledges. The duplicity of the several ministers, each striving to throw upon the others the responsibility of maintaining their official word, has kept me in continual attack upon them, by mail or telegram, since December last. But I shall hold them to it till they yield—if my strength holds out. When I see their orders in the hands of the collector here, I shall *believe*—and then I must hasten away from this climate. I hope in my next letter to tell you that every obstacle, official, priestly, and municipal, is removed—and that there actually is *no* check upon the admission of American publications, now waiting entrance on the border, as well as upon those hereafter to be granted.

Mr. Hale has been indefatigable in his interest in this work. Let American christians suitably acknowledge his noble service.

SEVILLE, APRIL 22, 1869. * * * I am happy to inform you that more than half the books are on Spanish soil ! Many of them already in circulation ! The balance just arrived, and in Custom House, awaiting farther orders from Madrid. So that *at last*, after four months application, and pressure, and correspondence ; after an unremitting contest with cardinals, bishops, priests,—to say nothing of adverse influences *in our own Legation*, the work is *accomplished*. Our abundant thanks are due Mr. Hale, and his secretary, Mr. Kinsley, for their unwearied and gentlemanly efforts in prosecuting this endeavor. I repeat the statement, that it may be remembered, and recognized at home.

SEVILLE, APRIL, 1869. * * * We now know what *has been* accomplished ; and we have had the satisfaction of rendering assistance to our Scotch and English friends here, for the same result, without which, themselves acknowledge they would still be powerless to do anything with the government. But I have nothing to guarantee for the future. Serano, in a magnanimous moment, made us a promise—and that promise has *at last* been ratified. Unquestionably, to my mind, he made it in good faith—but for the future, the pressure of the priesthood and the clamor of the opposition may oblige him, and the other members of the ministry, for reasons of public policy, to gain time by inertia. Whoever endorses Spanish official action without a proviso, is a fit candidate for a mad-house.

But *these* books are entered ! And could you witness the pleas for them, or the eagerness with which they are accepted, or the reverence with which they are folded between waiting hands,—you could better understand the significance of the words, *Bibles are now admitted into Spain.*

I need not assure you that official eyes rested with bitter malignity on every box, as they were passed through the port of Cadiz,—but I had *the order from Madrid in my hand,* and nothing could hinder them. But in Seville, where there is a second local customs ceremony, corresponding to the *octroi* in France —they met a different reception. When the freight arrived from Cadiz, I was at station to see that every case came through. The Spanish evangelists had one friend in the corps of officials, and they had expressed great apprehension over the possible tumult, in case he were not in service on the day the books were passed. One of them accompanied me that morning—who with feverish anxiety glanced over the group of officers—and them came to me with breathless haste, exclaiming, "Ah, Señor, he is *not* here ! There will be great trouble !" Preferring to get this timid soul off the ground, I sent him back to the city on an errand for myself—and then producing my papers, took *my* ground to watch proceedings. Box after box was handled by the employèes from car to platform—from platform to the waiting drays ; each receiving, as it passed, the close scrutiny of the officers of customs in attendance. Among these men, their chief particularly attracted my notice—for his fierce, almost fiendish expression and manner, while this work was going on. He looked the incarnate type of coming inquisition tortures. *I expected trouble with him.* But when the last box had been delivered—and passed—and the employèes and other officials had left the platform for other duties, his whole aspect instantly changed. Hurriedly looking

around to be sure of no witnesses to his confession, he walked
up to me, and laying his hand on my shoulder said, "Señor,
were there *Bibles* in those boxes?"—and then added, looking
steadily and earnestly into my eyes, "Is it possible, Señor, that
you are taking them all away without offering me one?"
Quickly taking one from my pocket, I gave it to him. His face
was transformed with a new light, as he seized it,—reverently
kissed the covers—and then, folding it to his heart, lifted his
streaming eyes to Heaven and said, "I thank thee, *mio Senor
Jesu Christo*, that this day I hold Thy sacred word in my
hands."

I cannot describe the joy of these Spaniards, who have been
praying and waiting for years for this blessing. I often think
of the multitudes of sons and daughters at home—yes, of
fathers and mothers, too—who are ashamed to manifest their
reverent interest in the Blessed Book—and are almost ashamed
to be seen reading it—for fear they shall be pronounced narrow
or fanatical.

On Saturday last, a leading citizen came into the ware-room,
where the books lay in *piles* on the floor, and said to me, "Ah,
my dear sir, my heart is full! Nowhere in my lovely country
have I ever witnessed so beautiful a sight as this!" Men and
women who have grown gray in unremitting service for souls,
taking their lessons by stealth from the concealed Word, now
take up a copy of the Bible and reverently hold it to their lips,
before they turn the pages. We are dispatching packages to
every part of the country—though we could use every copy in
this city alone. Bibles and other books, by the case, have gone
on to Madrid, Malaga, Cordova, and Grenada,—and more are
going to Valencia and Barcelona.

The editor of *El Betis*, one of the principal daily newspapers
of Cordova, a few days since made the following proposition to
the evangelists in that city : "Give me three hundred Testaments, and I will give you the privilege of inserting anything
you choose, not exceeding a column, in my paper. If you
accept my offer, I shall use the Testaments as prizes for new
subscribers." They have applied to me for the Testaments.
The first one hundred and fifty go into the editor's hands this
morning. Thus another liberal paper becomes a teacher of
simple truth as it is in Jesus.

Many thousands of hearts are made glad by your donations to Spain. Many thousands are pouring out their thanksgivings, who for many years have hungered and thirsted in vain for *the blessed word.*

BARCELONA, MAY 6, 1869. * * * The interest and life the *Estrella* music, and the Tract Society Primer give to the schools, is marvellous. Since our cases of books arrived, I have supplied for the opening of other Sabbath Schools in Seville,— and for similar schools in Cordova, Malaga, Madrid, and Huelva,—and have brought more with me to be used for that purpose in Valencia and this city. Mr. Lawrence is doing a great work here, and a large supply is much needed.

I find that the larger cities and towns throughout the south are adopting a system of free days schools, similar in some respects to our own, but they are without sufficient text-books. The books sent by the American societies have been dispatched into every province in Spain—but they are only crumbs among the starving. I sent, through Rev. Mr. T——, an offer to the Alcalde of Seville, to supply gratuitously, the Tract Primer for the infant classes in the day schools in that city, and after examination of a copy he most cordially *endorsed the book.*

Politically, this country is passing through deep waters. It is still a serious problem whether she finds anchorage, or whether she drifts at the mercy of wind and storm. In all that constitutes republicanism, she is making rapid progress—but is still at great distance from self-government.

GENEVA, SWITZERLAND, JULY, 1869. * * * Mr. T. writes me from Seville that while a colporter was selling books at one of the great Fairs, which occur throughout Spain at this season, he was arrested, and his books were taken from him, the officers alleging that the books *had never paid duty.* It was only necessary to go to the Custom House to prove the injustice of the charge—but while this was being done *in slow Spain,* the Fair closed. A new dodge of the priests !

Four priests in Seville have recently come out from the church of Rome, and seven other young men from the Roman Catholic University are also studying with Mr. F——, and are in preparation for pastoral labor. He expects, in the autumn, to open a large training school.

GENEVA, JULY, 1869. * * * The Pope, in a letter, of which telegraphic reports are just received, says : "The condition of the church in Spain severely afflicts me." Well it may. Spain is no longer bound, but the shackles remain, as also do those who would gladly re-apply them. The future freedom and glory of Spain lies, under Providence, *entirely* at the will of protestant christendom.

PARIS, AUGUST 7. * * * The work is going forward. A very promising enterprise is the voluntary organization of a society among the Spaniards themselves, to aid the poor, with provision of cheap dinners for the laboring classes.

The San Bernardo Evangelist writes from Seville : "There is one person who is not satisfied with all this work, and that is the parish priest. He calls us names, and sets on mobs of boys to stone our windows, and if possible to break up our meetings—but the people only laugh at him, and *come the more*."

NEW YORK, OCTOBER, 1869. * * * I regard the Spanish work as only just begun. The Bible and religious truth have been introduced—schools are established—churches are organized,—but in the present chaotic state of beliefs, there is great danger, if American christians neglect Spain, that her millions, like those of Italy, may drift back to infidelity and general unbelief.

NEW YORK, MARCH 23, 1870. * * * Yesterday, a year ago, we left Gibraltar, and had the chase across the Bay to reach the steamer—and also the sail by Tarifa, Trafalgar, and through the cross-seas of the Straits into Cadiz harbor : thence, *through the ordeal of the customs*, into the city—snatching the odd minutes to revisit the cathedral, churches, Alameda,—and the Capuchin convent—for one more look at Murillo's last painting, and found it draped for Holy Week. How the gardens abounded in flowers and sweet odors ! Then on Tuesday up to Seville—after that memorable fortnight of "perils by sea, and perils by land, and *perils by false brethren*."

Many of the facts received from Spain by Mr. Hall, after his return to America, were made public through the religious press of New York and Boston. Many others were embodied in "Occasional Papers" for private circulation among the liberal donors to that work in the Tabernacle Church. One letter, of many of most interesting character, received from Mr. Lawrence, and a few brief extracts from others, will close this testimony for Spain through her departed friend.

BARCELONA, MARCH 8, 1871. * * * My dear brother in the Lord. In the old city of Sarragossa there is a good work begun. About one thousand people come together to hear the gospel. In many other parts of the north there are evident signs of blessing. But we want men and means to take hold of the opening doors. Our schools greatly prosper. Surely it is a pleasant sight to see Spanish boys going to and from school with the Bible strapped among their school-books. Rome is alarmed, and sets up schools beside ours, but to no purpose. The parents remain firm, being convinced that their children receive a sounder education in our schools. I should be glad indeed if our American friends would help us with men and means, in this important work—and should be glad if you were stronger in body, to advocate Spain's claims. * * * My Bible work goes on most encouragingly. We visit towns and villages with the coach, and from time to time see most happy results. At Matero, a few weeks ago, while addressing the people from the stand, a young man, a traveller, came up and bought a Bible. He put it under his arm, and walking into the middle of the square, began to repeat aloud the 23d of Matthew. He did this, verse by verse. This gathered a great crowd. He then took out his Bible, and read the same chapter, addressing the people. We inquired about this strange proceeding. He told us that when we were there six months ago he bought a Bible, and gospel by Matthew,—that at home, his sister, influenced by the priests, *burned the Bible*,—that he saved the gospel by

Matthew, and learned that chapter—and that now he should guard his Bible. * * * One beautiful feature of the work in this city is, that we have no divisions. The whole work is one. I greatly rejoice in the unity. The Lord commands His blessing. This is the supreme moment for effort in these Roman empires, which are dissolving and breaking up. Now is the time to lay hold of the high places. There must of necessity come reaction—and a strong pull to regain the lost ; and before that comes, I feel that we must work well. This is the acceptable time for Spain. May the Lord bless you, strengthen you, and use you greatly for this work.

Believe me yours,   GEO. LAWRENCE.

* * * My manner of working is as follows : I have had constructed a large tent with flags and banners on which are texts such as *Dios es amor*—"God is love ;" *Christo Jesu sino al mundo*, etc.,—"God so loved the world," etc. This tent was first pitched at San Isidro, not far from Madrid, and near the hermitage of the patron saint of the latter city. As the thousands came out from the chapel whence they went to kiss the bone of their dead saint, they saw our texts, and came near for a closer inspection, and then to purchase. General Prim and Mayor Rivero seemed highly pleased with the new method of meeting the masses. * * *

* * * Alcalca, another city of priests, was surprised, at the Fair, by our novel tent. I was invited by the students to a discussion with padre C——. I went, and for two hours kept before them regeneration, sanctification by the Cross and the Holy Spirit, and the individual need of full assurance. These points they endeavored to avoid, and preferred *the Fathers*. I kept to the *Grandfathers*, Matthew, Mark, Luke, and John. They pressed the teachings of the church ; I plead the Living Word, and the unction of the Spirit. We parted good friends.

MADRID, 1870.—Prof. K. wrote. * * * One day, as I was writing in my study, I heard a sweet, plaintive, child's voice under my windows, singing one of those airs of Spain, half Oriental—half European. I was so much affected by the peculiar richness of the tones, that I sent my servant down to call the lad. I soon learned that he spent his time leading his blind father about the streets, to gain a few pennies to live by. So I induced his parents to let him come to our Sabbath School—and in time he suggested singing, in the thoroughfares, the pieces he had learned.   You can form an idea of the effect it produced to hear a poor little boy, leading a blind man along, singing in the busy street, "I know 'tis Jesus loves my soul."

I must tell you of a little fellow who wanted a Bible, but could not afford to buy one, as it cost nearly a shilling, (twenty cents,) and he earned only five pence (ten cents,) a day, which he needed for food and clothing. So what did he do ? *He went without his chocolate for seventeen days, and ate dry bread alone,* poor, dear boy ; he who at best had only bread and chocolate in the morning, and a dinner of little more. By this sacrifice he saved up three reals, (fifteen cents,) and came for a New Testament. Of course I gave him a *Bible,* and took his money, for I thought it not best to weaken the effect of the noble act.

* * * A fine young woman of twenty came to our meetings in San Cayetano. My attention was called to her strong, sweet voice in singing. Her whole soul seemed poured out in these beautiful hymns. Every night she attended,—and it was soon evident to me that she was one of those cases that pass silently into a believing state. In the presence of two evangelists I asked her, "Antonia, do you love the Saviour ?" "Oh, yes ! I live a new life, now." "Well, Antonia, did you always love Jesus ?" "I didn't know about Him, but as soon as I heard of Him, and that I could come to Him without paying a *cuarto*—just as I am—I did, and I've loved Him ever since." "Do you pray to Him ?" "Oh, yes, at home, at my work, anywhere." "But I want some proof that you are a changed person, Antonia. It is not words, you know, that save us." "All I can say is, *I feel God,"*—(*siento á Dios.*) "That will do," I replied with enthusiasm. In a few days after, she was rudely repulsed from her home, late at night, by the terrible epithets indeed in Spain, "Judia," "herige," (*Jewess, heretic*). She wandered up and down the streets in that dangerous ward, in the cold, malarious night air, when a poor Galician water-carrier, who knew her family, took her to his own home. The day following she was dismissed from her work in the factory, —but we soon got her restored. Now see the providence of God. In the Government Tobacco Factory were more than

5,000 women employed. We had often wanted to get the gospel among these women, as we do in the Government Hospitals, but they will not even suffer Spaniards to enter the building. More than one insurrection in Madrid has taken its rise in that building. One day Antonia came to us, asking for gospels and tracts to distribute there. We gave them—and now twenty to thirty of these fierce Amazons are constant attendants at our meetings.

APRIL, 1870. * * * I have now engaged a blind man—*who can see Jesus*, to go, conducted by another young man, with a Bible cart, through the chief promenades of the city. * * * I have also constructed a small tent, which is carried by two brethren, Francisco and Augustin. They go to a public square—unfold their tent, after permission, which is six feet square, and covered with precious portions of the Word. This brings the people together, and the sales, and occasions for testifying to the gospel, are wonderful. *Do send me Bibles.*

* * * During the last month, we have sold at our depot in Madrid and at the Fairs, nearly 10,000 Bibles and Gospels—and distributed more than 50,000 tracts. Prof. R. has in Madrid a training school to prepare young men for the ministry, and for Bible-readers, and three schools in which are more than one thousand children and adults under daily religious instruction.

Mr Lawrence has sold (at a nominal price,) during the year, since Bibles were admitted through the customs—more than 300,000 copies of Bibles and "portions"—nearly one third the number put in circulation in all India in ten years. So great is the hunger of this people for the Word.

VII.

Passing "Over."

"To lie down on some high peak of those old hills, in body as in spirit, close to the entrance to the promised land—where my brow might grow cool with the dews of Hermon, and the soft, south wind would come up to me with the music of Gennesaret. O! that would be pleasant!"

It is the beauty, the divinity of the gospel, that the deeper the sorrow, the fuller the consolation that it brings; the keener, the more exquisite the pain we suffer, so much the sweeter and richer the comfort, the peace, and finally the joy that is born of the very anguish of our grief. * * *

* * * Such a life does not end when it ceases to move and act before our eyes; it lives in us, not only as a memory but as a power; it lives through us, as every good and noble thing tends to reproduce itself.—*Rev. J. P. Thompson.*

That last winter on earth was one of peculiar fragrance. The "silver cord" was loosed. The spirit so intensely alive to the deepest interests of his many friends — so earnest in its hold on the promises, for his family, for the church, and for the world, was dropping one by one the fetters that bound it, and the home where it lingered for the heavenly call seemed, to those who entered it, and to those who dwelt there, like a portal to the house not made with hands.

(179)

His physicians were personal and devoted friends, — two of them very dear relatives — and all that professional skill, or undying affection could command, were offered to hold the precious life — but *the Master had need of him.*

He was surrounded by friends whose names, to his family, will be household words forever. Their constant and lavish gifts of the flowers he most loved, of the delicacies he most enjoyed, and of the little "surprises" that so enlivened his retired life, were keenly appreciated, and gratefully received.

One instance of this devotion may suitably be mentioned. In February, a sudden relish for eggs led him to request them one morning for his breakfast. The faithful Cornelius was sent hither and yon, along the avenues, without success. One grocer said he had been offered a dollar each for fresh ones, for invalids. Next day, he playfully mentioned this disappointment to gentlemen who called to see him. Presently, little baskets and boxes, with special garniture, began to come in — from Staten Island — from the homes along the Hudson — from private stables in the city — and even from Bennington, Vt. — till at the close of that week, *five dozens* had been acknowledged. They were too many for the invalid, but they all brought the odor of frankincense and myrrh, and not one was appointed to common use. In little parcels, they went out to other sick chambers, with his smiling benediction. One city coachman continued for many weeks to bring a few, three times weekly. He was told of the abundance. "Excuse me," said Joseph, "I have orders to keep Mr. Hall supplied with fresh eggs, and *I must claim the privilege.*

Lily of the Valley, was known among his friends as his favorite flower — though only his family knew it was associated with his mother's memory — and from January, when it graced a bouquet of superb roses that were sent him with New Year greetings, that flower was always remembered in the fresh supplies that almost daily filled his room, and the house, with choice odors — till, on that last morning in April, a cluster of its fragrant bells were laid on his unconscious breast.

But more than all, he lived in his communion with the saints — in his fellowship with the working element of the church. His deepest, most earnest plans had been for *young men.*

In these last months, he carried them one by one, day after day and night after night, to the mercy-seat, in supplication that seemed inspired. He held his interest in individuals to the last, — mentioning them *by name* in his petitions, but his quickened vision embraced them all, throughout our own and other lands, that they might "grow into the stature of perfect ones in Christ Jesus," so that the great work of elevating the world might gain force *mightily* with the present and incoming generations.

On the first Sabbath in March, of that year, his two elder sons were received into the fellowship of the Tabernacle Church. The tender, tearful service at the altar, and the loving pastor's prayer of dedication were preceeded in *the sunny " blue room,"* in Forty-Third street, by a committal even more tenderly impressive, when, with his children kneeling by his bed-side, he laid a wasted hand on each dear head, and poured out his soul for covenant blessings on them all, and " upon children's children, to the latest generation." *

This fragment from manuscript lines, found

---

* On the fifth anniversary of that occasion — March 3, 1878—the youngest son was also received into the fellowship of the same church.

among his memoranda after death, will express
his depth of feeling on that occasion :

> * * * Ah, pure of face !
> Ah, high of mien !
> The dearest vision I have seen !
> With covenant-seal firm set in prayer,
> With covenant-bond deep graven there,
> All gifts they consecrate *to Him*
> *Whose life was consecrate to them.*
> So lithe of limb—
> So clear of sight,—
> So happy in their youthful might,
> So strong to do the Master's will,—
> So glad their mission to fulfill !
> With calm, unwavering trust to-day,
> They enter on the narrow way ;
> And kneeling at the altar now
> Our darlings take the solemn vow.
> * * * * * * * *
> * * * Guard thou their steps where'er they roam,
> From " morning dew "
> To " even-tide,"
> Let them through all the way abide,
> Close by thy side ! close by thy side !
> Dear Christ the Lord ! the crucified !

With tears, he said one day to Dr. Taylor,
whose constant visits were a great delight to
him, "Oh, how I should like to live to work
with you for the young men of New York !
They have a great work before them of good or
evil ! *God grant it may not be evil.* All that
talent must be consecrated ! "

His last efforts with his pen were made with
difficulty, but from his bed, letters were exchanged

with the Presidents of New England Colleges, concerning a plan of scholarships to be sustained by the home church. His last hours were happier that these new avenues to learning, and influence were thus opening, to some who might never find others of equal breadth.

One sunny morning, in April, his face took on new radiance. The "golden bowl" was breaking. "I have made a mistake all my life ; *living* is the valley of the shadow of death, — *dying is going home.*"

"I have no anxiety about my boys, as to education, whether or not they go through college, — so that they become *noble, high-minded, useful christian men.*"

"If it were my last word to them," referring to young men in whose personal success he felt a deep interest, "it would be to fasten their faith *to the Rock Christ Jesus,* and all will be well with them."

"I feel weak — I cannot say much — but this I know and believe — "*the communion of saints, the resurrection of the body, and the life everlasting.*"

"It is only a shallow stream, and *Christ is on the other side!* Do not dread it when you come. *It is nothing to go over.*"

And the freed spirit went *over* into the life of unending activities.

> " ' Sometime ' we say, and turn our eyes
>   Toward the far hills of paradise—
> 'Some day '—'sometime,' a sweet new rest
>   Shall blossom, flower-like, in each breast.
> Sometime—some day—our eyes shall see
>   The faces kept in memory.
> Some day their hands shall clasp our hands
>   Just over in the morning lands."

There was a very simple service over the dear remains, in the home forever hallowed by the baptism of his saintly life, — and then he was carried, by loving hands, to the church he had served so long — where, amid flowers, and sweet anthems, and tender prayers, and bitter tears, — old and young — rich and poor — looked their last upon his beloved face.

The same evening, just as the full moon rose over the Western Massachusetts hills, he was silently taken from the train at Whately, once more over the threshold of the dear home "under the elms," where, as an invalid, he had spent so many delightful days, — and there, next morning, the village pastor, with broken voice, repeated the promises to those who wept over him — and many who had honored him in life,

12

sang songs of gratitude and consolation. At evening, in the little church at Ashfield, his valued friend, the Rector of St. Johns, conducted the tender committal service — and those who loved him from his boyhood, laid him gently to the long rest, under the shadow of old "Sunny-side," his favorite mountain. In the quiet village cemetery, the first light of day breaks over his grave — and her last loving smile lingers at evening farewell.

> * * * There let him lie !
> Where sentinel-spirits tenderly tread.
> Let roses, and "daisies," and sunshine, and "grasses,"
> Wave over his bed.
> Then when he awaketh, a spirit redeemed,
> A glorified essence, more pure than he seemed,
> Or mortal hath dreamed—
> Far in the hereafter, faith changing to sight,
> He will walk with the saints, on the mountains of light,
> In garments of white !

Rev. Mr. Wells, of Montreal, and Rev. A. H. Clapp, D. D., of New York, shared the tender Tabernacle services over their friend, — and after allusions to his specific city work in Church and Mission Schools, Rev. Dr. Taylor said :

What a blessed thing it is that we are able to appropriate with the fullest assurances the consolations of the gospel, in regard to the beloved brother whose remains now lie before us ! I may not presume to speak of him with the same free-

dom as those could use who have known him during all the
years of his christian course ; and even while I refer to the
impressions produced upon me by his character and deportment
during the brief year in which I was permitted to call him
friend, I would desire to do so in the spirit of his own words.
"If," said he, "anything is said over me, after I am gone, let it
be said of Christ." Let us therefore glorify Christ in him. We
glorify Christ for what he made his servant. He was a member of the Bible class of Deacon Pitts, whose name is still as
ointment poured forth, to many in connection with the Broadway Tabernacle Church. Mr. Hall was one of a large number
of young men whom that devoted christian was instrumental
in leading to the Lord, and when in October, 1851, he made a
public profession of allegiance to Jesus, "he dedicated himself," as he has frequently said since, "to the Lord, with a desire to make himself specially useful to young men, both because of the dangers to which in such a city as this they are
exposed, and because of the valuable service they might render
to the Redeemer's cause." Ye are witnesses, my brethren, how
steadily during all these years the Lord enabled him to keep to
this resolution, and there are many here to-day who are living
testimonies to the success which he achieved. To this end his
heart was with young men, and his constant prayer was that
many of them might be brought in. The last time he was out
he came to my study to talk with me concerning the revival of
the young men's Sabbath morning class, and when during
these months of weakness he expressed any desire for life, his
main object in that was that he might continue to work in
Christ. What a joy it was to him, when on the first Sabbath
of last March his two elder sons publicly united with the
church ! and how eagerly he looked forward to coming days
of ingathering in this church, those who saw him often in his
latest days can testify ! But it was not for young men only
that he cared. He was mainly instrumental in establishing the
mission-school in 54th street years ago, and in all matters con-
nected with the Bethany Mission he ever manifested the most
eager interest. He was the counselor of all the young workers
engaged in it, and if in coming years any large success shall be
given to us here, much of it I am certain will come in answer
to the prayers which he so fervently offered in its behalf.

To the poor also he was a constant minister. I had not been two days on these shores when he came to me and gave me a list of the poorer members of the church, commending them to my tender attentions, and often when I have gone among them, I have heard his name mentioned by them with the most fervent benediction. It was true of him as of the ancient patriarch, "When the ear heard him then it blessed him, when the eye saw him then it gave witness to him because he delivered the poor and him that had no helper." Indeed, more than almost any man with whom I have come into contact, he seemed to live and move and have his being in the prosperity of the church of Christ. He came as near as a mere man could come I think, to an embodiment of the fine lines in Dr. Dwight's well known hymn,

> For her my tears shall fall,
> For her my prayers ascend,
> To her my cares and toils be given
> Till toils and cares shall end.
> Beyond my highest joy
> I prize her heavenly ways,
> Her sweet communion, solemn vows,
> Her hymns of love and praise.

Nor was it only at home that he bestirred himself for Christ. Wherever he was, he was on the out-look for opportunities of doing good. When, in search of health, he went in 1861 to Spain, he did every thing that he could, in the boldest and most fearless manner, to commend Christ to those with whom there he came into contact. He was not ashamed of the chain of Matamoras, and in the face of a scowling multitude he and a friend went and took the brave confessor by the hand, as he was being taken to his prison. On a subsequent visit to the same country after the revolution, he was the first to introduce the Scriptures into it, and so earnest was he in this effort that when we warned him that he might lose his life in his labors he replied, "I would be willing to die if I could only get these Bibles into the country."

His labors at that time were instrumental in interesting the members of the Tabernacle Church in Spanish Evangelization, and undoubtedly prepared the way for the step which has recently been taken by the American Board, in instituting missions in Spain and other papal countries. Thus "he being dead," will yet "speak," through the Lawrences, the Gulicks, and others who are devotedly working in that interesting field.

But while from personal reasons he was peculiarly drawn to Spain, his heart went out to missionaries all over the world. The monthly missionary concert was always a great occasion with him, and not seldom in his last months of weakness he would write a short note with a few missionary gleanings, to be read by the leader of the meeting. Thus alike in his prayers and his efforts, he was in full sympathy with Him who has taught us to say, "Thy kingdom come, Thy will be done in earth as it is in Heaven."

His last years were full of weakness and of suffering as well as of labor. To use his own expression, he walked for years by the side of his own open grave, but the Good Shepherd was with him, and His rod and staff comforted him. He was sometimes depressed and prone to look on the dark side of things, but the depression never extended for a moment to spiritual things. He said again and again, "There is not a shadow, there is not a doubt. It is all peace." And his thoughts were continually tending upwards to his heavenly home. When a friend had sent him some beautiful flowers, he said, "They are very beautiful and very fragrant, but I shall soon be where everlasting spring abides and never withering flowers. * * * When on the day before his death I asked him how he was, he replied, "nearer home."

These are very precious sayings. Let us thank the Lord Jesus for thus sustaining His servant, and as each one is saying, "let my last end be like his," let us all remember that only to them to whom it is Christ to live, is it given to have such experiences when they come to depart.

From the many letters received by his family after his death, a few brief extracts are offered, as a closing tribute to this earnest and fragrant life :

New Haven, April 16, 1873. * * * 'He passed away, leaving behind him, I am proud to think, no better man.' Thus

Thomas Hughes writes in his ' Memoirs of a Brother,' just published, and when I read that sentence four or five weeks ago, away in Italy, I said to myself, ' thus all who know my friend, Mr. Hall, will feel, when he passes from earth.' There is great comfort in the thought of what he was ; * * * great satisfaction that the slender thread of life was kept so long from breaking. * * * It is amazing to me that one so good and true, one so diligent in the great service, one so zealous in every good work, should find so much merit in others, as he did. * * * I have no particulars yet—but shall seek them from friends in New York.

ANDOVER, MASS., APRIL 16, 1873. * * * I have just received a note from my father telling me that my beloved brother in the Lord has gone home. I saw he was failing when I was last in New York, and felt that I should not see him again, though he spoke of Ashfield and the summer. Bless the Lord who has spared him so long to His people here ; and now has taken him to the prepared mansions to await his friends. What joy to him ! and to us who remain, how rich the treasure there ! * * * What joy to have had so long fellowship with one of the saints in light ! What joy that he is waiting now with the love and the knowledge of the glorified ! * * * The dear Lord who wept with the little household at Bethany shall give you His tender consolation."

IPSWICH. * * * Such a husband and father to hold on to in memory and faith, is the next best thing to his personal presence. He is gone, but not dead ! His heavenly experiences have not shut up his earthly loves. * * *

NEW YORK. * * * Being dead, he whom we all loved so well yet speaketh. How well I remember the last prayer-meeting he attended in the Tabernacle chapel, and *the prayer he offered*, inspired as it seemed by his nearness to the world unseen. May God graciously bless and guide us all, that we may follow him who has now "entered in through the gates, into the city."

MONTREAL. * * * What blessed memories of faithful service we have to look back upon. If earthly privileges and opportunities are *ever* improved, it fell to his lot to improve them *to the utmost*. These are memories for ages to come.

BEAVER ST., NEW YORK. * * * If at any time, or in any way, I can *ever* be of service you háve but to command. It is the only way in which I can ever be able to acknowledge obligations of personal kindness and advice received through a series of years, from him whose lips are forever sealed.

NEW YORK. * * * * (Alluding to the burial services.) "How sweet and fragrant and precious it all was! What a legacy to the children to have it to remember how much of tenderness and love and respect were lavished upon their honored father. * * * I know they will have all the comfort there is—all that this world can give, and all that heavenly messengers can bring. * * How very touching and beautiful the reception in W., at that evening hour! what an alleviation! what a prophecy! what a symbol!" * * *

* * * "In your great sorrow it seems to me that you have the two chief consolations,—the spotless memory of your husband and the noble promise of his sons. * * * It is fortunately part of the immortality of human goodness that it leaves a perpetual benediction upon the places that knew it, so that they acquire a deeper beauty and a subtler charm. In that sense it is the presence only that has gone to the eyes, not to the heart and the life. * * * May his serene and smiling faith sustain your own."

* * * "I can only assure you that the cloud now passing over your home also casts its shadow over our dwelling. We regard him with almost reverent affection, so faithfully has he served his generation and his God. I have had some opportunity to study his character, and I can say in all sincerity it has inspired me with profound respect and admiration. The clearness of his intuitions—the soundness of his judgment—his prompt fidelity to his convictions of duty—his untiring activity in christian philanthropic labors, even in his feebleness, and his tender interest in his friends, have made him, in my esteem, a model of christian manhood. * * *

* * * We have all reason for gratitude that he has been spared so long,—especially that the young enjoyed so long his counsels, and witnessed his example. May his mantle fall on them! may his prayers be answered! and his hopes be realized by a similar consecration of their lives to the service of the Divine Master."

IN MEMORIAM.

HENRY CLAY HALL.

Fell aslëep April 12, 1873.

Aged 45 Years.

At a Regular Business Meeting of the Broadway Tabernacle Church, held on Wednesday evening, April 30th, 1873, the clerk made official announcement of the death of DEACON HENRY C. HALL, and presented the following communication from the Church Committee, which was unanimously adopted by the Church:

WHEREAS it has pleased God in his wisdom to remove from the Church Militant to the Church Triumphant, our beloved brother HENRY CLAY HALL, for twenty-two years a member of this Church, and for more than ten years one of its deacons, this church desire to place upon record their appreciation of his exemplary character and many virtues, and of the services rendered by him to it, and to the cause of Christ in the world. Always in the place where duty called him, so long as health and strength permitted, he has during his long and wearisome sickness set us an example of patient suffering, and has shown by efforts which few are disposed to make even in the flush of health, what one loving disciple of Christ, when thoroughly consecrated to his service, can do for the advancement of his kingdom and for the good of souls. This church will miss the prayers and active labors of our dear brother, and that busy brain of his always contriving some new plan for doing good, or some new means of pressing forward in work already begun ; the church committee will miss his wise counsels, and loving conciliatory spirit ; our young men will mourn the loss of a kind, judicious adviser, whose words always carried weight as coming from a heart filled with love ; all who love our Lord Jesus Christ will miss one who was ever foremost in every good word and work.

* * * We rejoice that he has ceased to bear the cross, and shall henceforth wear the crown ; we thank God for another added to the number of those who have departed this life in His faith and fear, and whose works do follow them, and we pray that God may enable us and all who loved our brother, to follow him, as he followed Christ, and to pay to his memory the tribute which he would have most desired, in bringing forth much fruit for the Master.

www.ingramcontent.com/pod-product-compliance
Lightning Source LLC
Chambersburg PA
CBHW031104020726
4749SCB00007B/2035